BLOOD REVENGE

The men who had ambushed Buck had gone, probably split up. If he followed them close, they might wait for him, take him easy.

Buck drew breath, forced his blood to stop racing in his veins. He wanted them, wanted them bad, but this was not the time. This was their country, not his. They knew the land, he did not. But he had heard a voice speaking in the Spanish tongue. There was a curl to the accent that Buck recognized, from Texas, from his own rides south of the border.

So, the Californio was probably a Mexican.

But, who was he?

Buck didn't know, but he meant to find out.

When he did, he would kill him.

THE HOTTEST SERIES IN THE WEST CONTINUES!

PISTOLERO
BY WALT DENVER

ZEBRA BOOKS
KENSINGTON PUBLISHING CORP.

ZEBRA BOOKS

are published by

KENSINGTON PUBLISHING CORP.
475 Park Avenue South
New York, N.Y. 10016

First printing: February, 1984

Printed in the United States of America

For my sister Kay, and all the Bells: John, Kay, Rinzai, Jackie, Tzena, and Greymuira.

PROLOGUE

The men sat on the porch at Tanner's Saloon. Every one of them itched to stir up something. Trouble or fun, it didn't make much difference.

The afternoon sun had finally drifted over the roof and left them in welcome shadow. But they were bored and the beer was hot. The whiskey was rough as a cob and burned from tongue to asshole.

"Worst tanglefoot ever a man swallered," said one of them.

"Tanner!" yelled another.

A man in an apron pushed through the batwing doors. His hair drifted away from his forehead like weeds in a flash-flooded creek bed, straggly, thin strands slick with sweat. Tanner's hands shook because the men had been drinking hard all day and none of them had paid a damned dime yet.

"Yes sir, Mister Fowler. You want some more beer?" asked Joe Tanner. The politeness in his voice belied his dark thoughts.

"Green as shit, Tanner," said the man called

7

Fowler. "Green as hay shit."

The men on the porch guffawed. Tanner's face paled as if the sun was still out there lighting up the sand hills, the stones of the empty land. The saloon had the advantage of being out in the middle of nowhere. Monihans, Texas. But it also had the advantage of being in a lawless clutter of buildings they called a town. There was no sheriff in Monihans to listen to complaints. Men wore guns and they shot them when and where they pleased.

"Sorry about that, Mister Fowler. Last batch didn't turn out too good and I didn't have time to let it age. . . ."

"That ain't my big complaint," said Fowler, his lumpy face working up to a slit-eyed rage. "This whiskey's got too many chili peppers in it."

Fowler held up a half-empty bottle.

"And the terbacky's rank as buffler wool. What'd you do, Tanner, drag your shit-stained shorts through it?"

The men laughed again, louder than before.

They had ridden in early that morning, used up all of Tanner's water, put away the eggs and bacon, the beefsteaks, before starting in on the whiskey and beer. Fowler and the half dozen others. All men in their mid-thirties, Kansas men with leathered skin and flicking eyes that told Tanner they were hunted and would be hunted for as long as they rode, in whichever direction.

"I buy that whiskey, Mister Fowler. From a drummer what . . ."

"Go get us some good stuff, Tanner. If the next

8

bottle ain't better'n this coal oil I'm gonna make you drink your own poison."

Tanner backed through the bat-wings, shaking visibly.

"They's one!" announced a lean man at the edge of the porch. All eyes looked in the direction he pointed.

"Your shot, Fowler."

Fowler drew his converted Remington .44 pistol quickly. The lizard flicked its tail, moved its head in a sudden sideways motion. Fowler cocked the single-action, took aim. He held the sights just a touch low.

He took a breath, held it. Squeezed the trigger. The muffled bellow of ignited black powder filled the silence.

White smoke billowed out from the end of the barrel.

The lead ball spang-whined off the rock.

The smoke fell apart, blew away, and the lizard's body hung on the rock, its tail twitching and quivering as if still alive.

The lizard's head was gone. In its place a powdery mark on the rock about as big as a nickel.

"Got him clean."

"Puts you ahead, Fowler."

The men had been shooting lizards for the past hour. Shooting their heads off. Making bets. It didn't count if you shot the lizard off the rock. Or if you hit it in the body or tail. You had to shoot its head off clean. Some money changed hands now as Tanner came back out on the porch carrying a fresh bottle of whiskey.

Fowler ejected the empty hull, working the ramrod under the barrel. He slipped a fresh shell in the cylinder. The man next to him picked up the brass, stuck it in his pocket. Fowler spun the cylinder to the empty one, eased the hammer down. He hefted the Remington in his hand as if still looking for something to shoot.

"Here's the best bottle I got in the house, Mister Fowler," said Tanner.

Fowler took the bottle, held it up to the light. The liquid swirled with bits and chunks of foreign matter. The label read: TANNER'S FINEST, Distilled Spirits. The whiskey was clear except for the bits of brown stuff floating in it.

"Probably made with worms and scorpions," said Fowler.

"I buy it from a drummer," said Tanner. "He puts my label on it."

"I bet it's real aged, Tanner. At least twelve hours old."

Tanner paled again. Fowler had not holstered his pistol. It now lay handy in his lap.

"I'll ask the drummer . . ."

"Oh, dry up, Tanner," Fowler interrupted. "We'll pull the cork on this in a few minutes. If I let out a howl, you come runnin'." Fowler's lumps shifted places on his face, but his porker eyes gleamed with warning.

Tanner went back inside the saloon.

Scaggs, the man on the end of the porch, stood up, unbuttoned his fly. He walked a step and urinated off the end of the porch. The urine steamed yellow craters in the dust.

"You use that pecker a lot, Scaggs," drawled a red-headed Kansas with off-set eyes.

"I use it when necessary, Bob-Joe," snapped Scaggs.

"You get to enjoy the beer twice't. Once when you guzzle it, and again when you play with your pecker."

"I ain't playin' with it, Bob-Joe."

"Shake it more'n once, you are," said a scar-faced man named Phelps who shared a crude bench made of pine with Bob-Joe Morgan.

Laughter rippled from whiskey-slaked throats.

Scaggs shook his penis out, tucked it back in his trousers. He sat down, looked out over the baked land. It was time for another lizard to come out and try to sun on one of the stones.

"Reckon we gonna pay Tanner?" asked Scaggs.

"Not if we can help it," interjected Big Bill Johnson, this thick legs dangling over the porch. His boots were unshined, worn and scarred, patches of leather missing. "Right, Fowler?"

"Likely we'll draw some pay for ourselfs after having to swallow this rotgut," said Fowler, grinning lop-sided. His face looking bee-stung because he did not live well and because he had once been a pretty fair saloon brawler.

Two lizards slithered onto the rocks, blinked in the sun.

Two pistols boomed and the lizards disappeared as if they had been only imaginery.

Smoke hung in the air and it was quiet for a few moments.

11

"What're you gonna do, Joe?" Angie Tanner asked her husband. "They ain't gonna pay."

Tanner tried to push his wife back inside the kitchen. His nerves clattered as the shots outside seemed to resonate in the walls of the adobe room.

"I'm worried what's gonna happen when Billy and Turk Nolan came riding in after work."

Billy was their son. Eighteen years old, hot-headed and wild. Turk was the same age, but cooler.

"Maybe those men will be gone by then."

"No. They won't leave until evening. After the sun goes down. Those kind don't ride across Texas in daylight."

"No, I speck not. Well, they's a new boy joined with Billy and Turk yesterday."

"I know, Angie. He won't be no trouble. Quiet sort."

"Except for his eyes, Joe. He's got real restless eyes."

Joe Tanner looked at his wife with an expression of impatience.

"What's that supposed to mean? He's got eyes same as anyone else."

"Hazel eyes. Green-like. Deep."

"You looked real close, Angie."

"Can't forget those eyes." She busied herself with putting away washing plates. "He talks polite and all, but you can tell by the eyes. He'll get riled real easy, I'm thinkin'."

"Hush that kind of talk. There's not gonna be no trouble here. We'll speak to the boys, tell 'em what kind of men those are out there."

Tanner watched his short, rotund wife stretch to put up the plates. He could have helped, but it was her job. She would have resented it. At least he had her in the kitchen where her voice couldn't be heard by those on the porch. It was hot in there and the sun blazed through the windows with the force of a blast furnace. He didn't know how she could stand it.

Angie walked to the back door, opened it. This only made the room seem hotter, more glaring. She leaned against the jamb, lifted a frazzle of hair that had strayed down her cheek, began twining it around her finger.

The sun framed her in silhouette, backlit her strawberry hair.

" 'Sides," Tanner said, as if responding to a question she had asked, "that whelp's just a boy. Younger'n Billy."

"Not by much. Year or two."

"Makes all the difference. He say what his name was?"

"Turk called him Buck. Jess Buck."

"Where'd he come from?"

Angie shrugged, flapped her apron like a fan.

"Billy didn't say."

Well, you catch those boys a-comin', you try and send 'em on home."

Tanner looked past his wife to the flat plain, the expanse of sand. A place where nothing grew but cactus and sagebrush, mesquite and greasewood. The boys were working at a ranch in the Pecos river Valley, half a day's ride from the saloon. This was Saturday and they'd be riding in before the sun went down. They had passed by yesterday, unexpectedly, after delivering twenty head of beef to Odessa the day before.

More shots sounded from the front porch. Tanner winced, but Angie stepped out of the doorway, leaned against the wall, in shadow.

"Where's my fan?" she asked.

"Oh, damn your fan," Joe Tanner grumbled, turning to go back into the saloon. It was just too damned hot in the kitchen and the beans simmering on the stove smelled sour. This day had started out all wrong and it didn't look as if it was going to turn out half-right either.

"Race you to the saloon," said Billy, a towheaded youth with the last of his freckles peppering his boyish face. His battered hat sat on his head at a rakish angle, worn with pride, weighing more than it should because he refused to shake out the dust.

"Aw, you show-off!" snapped Turk, a heavyset young man with permanently bowed legs, brown hair and a wad of plug tobacco bulging his cheek.

" 'Fraid to lose. Buck, you wanna race me?"

Buck rode a few yards behind the other two youths. He was younger, but looked older around the eyes. His hair was black, his eyes hazel: brown flecked with gold. When the light hit them a certain way, they shimmered a dull green. His face was smooth, with crisp outlines at the jaw and cheekbones. His nose was straight, etched just as hard as his jawline. He shook his head, said nothing.

Billy shrugged as he turned and saw Buck shaking his head. He had already decided that Buck didn't want to make friends. He was a hard worker, but didn't say much. He and Turk had tried to warm him up, but Buck never told them where he came from nor where he was going. It was just understood that he would work the ranch until he got enough money to go on to the next place. Wherever that was.

"Turk, you gonna race or not?"

"Hell, you wanna put up a bet on it?"

"A dollar, same as always."

"Two dolls and you give me two lengths."

"Get movin'," grinned Billy Tanner.

Turk dug his spurs into his horse's flanks, whopped the brindle on the rump. Billy's roan bolted as soon as Turk's horse leaped out in front of him. Beyond, they could just see the top of the saloon, the logs jutting through the adobe near the sod roof.

Billy yelled, kicked his horse.

Jess Buck watched them ride off, allowed himself a slow grin. His teeth were even, white. One of the eyeteeth was chipped, testifying to the fact that he'd had to bite a bullet at least once. He ran his tongue over the uneven edge now, and licked his lips.

That's when he heard the shots.

"Tanner! Get your ass out here!" roared Fowler.

Tanner came through the bat-wings as if shot from the saloon.

"Yessir?"

"Horse piss!"

"Huh?"

"This bottle tastes like horse piss. Taste it!"

The men on the porch seemed to draw closer together as Tanner took the bottle from Fowler.

"I—I don't drink hard likker," stammered Tanner.

Fowler drew his pistol.

"Drink it, barkeep, or I'll air your guts out right now."

Tanner, his face drained of blood, his hand shaking, brought the bottle to his lips. He raised it, let some of it trickle into his mouth. He gagged. The men laughed.

Fowler stood up, shoved Tanner off the porch with a single bat of his fisted hand. He might as well have been swatting a fly. The saloon owner stumbled, held onto the bottle.

The men stared down at Tanner. None of them looked friendly.

"Drink a big swaller," said Fowler quietly.

Tanner gulped, his Adam's apple quivering.

He tilted the bottle up to his lips.

Fowler started shooting at that instant. Ball lead spurted up dust near Tanner's shoes. He gagged again, spluttered. Then vomited.

"Jesus," said Bob-Joe.

Then, all the men drew pistols. They began shooting at Tanner's feet. He screamed. Choked. His shirt and vest were stained with half-digested lunch. His apron was soiled with yellow and red smears. Dust stung his ankles.

Angie came running through the bat-wings, saw the smoke and her husband. She screamed.

Billy Tanner and Turk Nolan rode around the corner of the building, hell-bent for leather.

"Hey, stop that!" yelled Billy.

The pistols fell silent. Smoke curled lazily from a half dozen barrels.

"Well, looky here," drawled Fowler. "A couple of desperadoes."

Laughter from the rest of the men on the porch.

Billy didn't think anything was funny. Turk looked as if he wanted to find a hole, crawl in, pull it in behind him. But he was stuck there and he didn't move.

"What're you doin' to my pa?" demanded Billy.

"Why, is that yore pa, boy?" said Fowler, leering at Billy, as he began ejecting hulls from his cylinder. The noise of the ejector made Turk wince. Fowler shoved in new bullets without ever glancing down at his pistol. He stared straight at young Billy Tanner.

"You leave him alone!"

Fowler shoved his pistol back in its holster. He kept his hand close to the butt. He stepped back a pace, spread his legs.

"Make me, boy."

"Billy, don't!" pleaded his mother in a hoarse whisper.

Joe Tanner looked at his son in horror.

Billy's face was contorted with rage. His mouth was drawn up, his eyes narrowed to angry puffed slits.

"It's all right, Billy," he said, his voice raspy from vomiting. "It don't mean nothin'."

Billy looked at the hardcases. They returned his stare with steely eyes. Turk started to back his horse, turn it.

"Hold steady there, son," said Scaggs, stepping forward. "You don't want to make any sudden moves right now."

Joe Tanner started to walk toward Billy.

Scaggs fired a round in the dirt, just in front of the bartender.

"You hold steady, too, Tanner."

Jess Buck rode up, seemingly in no hurry. His eyes seemed to take in everything at a single glance. He saw the drawn guns, a shaking Turk, Billy just about to explode, Mrs. Tanner on the porch looking as if someone had stolen all her pies, and Joe Tanner looking up at Billy like he was praying to himself.

The men looked up at Buck, as if surprised. Buck slid out of his saddle without being asked, walked to Billy's horse, touched the youth's leg.

Billy looked down at his new companion.

"You stay out of this," he said curtly.

Buck said nothing. Instead, he punched Billy's horse in the flank, slapped the animal's rump. The horse bunched his muscles, bolted away before Billy could rein him in.

Fowler's hand dove for his pistol.

Buck went into a crouch before anyone realized he had seen Fowler's move. His hand flashed like a kingfisher's shadow toward his pistol. A big Colt's .44, what they called The Peacemaker, appeared in his hand.

He was faster than anyone expected.

Faster than Fowler.

Fowler's pistol was half out of the leather when Buck fired. No one had even seen him cock the single action. The pistol seemed part of his hand. He pointed at Fowler and sparks, flame, smoke, belched from the barrel.

Fowler's left eye disappeared. Blood gushed out of the empty socket.

Scaggs, reacting faster than the others, swung his pistol on Buck.

Buck thumbed back the hammer, moved his barrel slightly, squeezed the trigger. His Colt boomed and bucked in his hand.

Others brought pistols up.

Buck fired again and again.

Four men fell, twitching.

Phelps backed away. So did Bob-Joe.

Another man, the one they called Cowlick, because of a tuft of hair that stuck out from under his hat at right angles to his face, shook his head. The downed men stopped twitching. Blood pools formed on the porch, settled. Flies swarmed to drink the warm fluid.

"They're all stone dead," said Tanner, in awe.

"You got one bullet left, or two?" asked Bob-

Joe. His eyes shifted to the other two men still standing.

Buck stayed in his crouch. His left hand hovered over the hammer of his cocked pistol.

"Some say it's dangerous to carry a full cylinder with a six-gun," the young man said quietly.

"One, then. Boys, we can take him." Bob-Joe Morgan didn't move however.

Phelps thought about it.

Cowlick went for it.

Buck shot him in the throat. A pink spray spattered Bob-Joe's cheek.

Phelps got as far as getting his hand on the butt of his pistol.

Buck shot him between the eyes. His skull came apart, spattered the bat-wing doors with bone and blood.

Bob-Joe shot his hands straight up in the air.

"You got seven shots in that gun, sonny?" he blurted.

Buck thumbed the hammer to half-cock, started pushing out empty shells with the plunger. He slid in fresh bullets. He did it all fast, without ever seeming in a hurry. Bob-Joe didn't even try to outguess the young man.

"I always carry six," said Buck, "and make sure nobody jars me."

CHAPTER ONE

Jess Buck let the lineback dun have its head while he stood up in the stirrups to look around.

He lazed his tongue over his nicked tooth. A thing he did when he was worried or nervous. Like now.

He looked back over his shoulder. Up ahead.

He saw nothing. Nothing that moved. Nothing that could be seen.

But for the past two or three miles he could have sworn someone was following him, watching him.

It was just a feeling.

A hard, strong feeling, like the tip of a knife at the base of the skull. Like a breathing in a dark empty room.

He knew the trail was used by horse thieves. Two way horses were sold in Prescott and Los Angeles. Sometimes again and again. Billy Edwards and Turk Reeve had told him about it back in Prescott. They were private hired, by breeders, to catch thieves, and it wasn't cared whether they brought any to trial. Good boys, tough as they come. They had told him to be careful. And, something else, too. But, he had been drinking and whatever they had said had reached him when he was wool-headed and fuzzy-tongued.

But the memory of those two came back to him now — and he wondered if they were behind him somewhere. Someone was.

And he had a hunch that someone was sure as hell watching him.

Buck believed in hunches.

He'd had a powerful number of them in the last ten years. In those years, since he'd killed his first man at Tanner's Saloon, he'd both hunted and been hunted. He knew the feeling.

He settled back in the saddle, reined the lineback in. Just in case. The land seemed to move slowly around him as he rode, changing sharply as he headed deeper into the high desert. The yucca and joshua trees began to dot the landscape. The slender yucca were in bloom, served as sentinel posts for the quail that roamed the cactus, sage-dotted land in scurrying coveys. Lizards glided silently from the warm rocks as his horse struck rock with shod hooves.

In the years since had killed the men at Tanner's and rode on, Buck had grown tall, leaned out. He topped six feet and his shoulders set wide and square on a spare frame without an ounce of fat on it. He chewed on an unlit cigar to keep his mouth moist, for it was blazing hot even that early in the spring. Water was scarce in this part of the country, what they called the Mojave

Desert, and he had a ways before he reached Twenty-nine Palms, the next water hole.

Buck felt the hot sun wetting his back and was glad he was heading west over San Gorgonio Pass instead of back across the Mojave. Some parts of California lived up to the name Hernan Cortez was said to have given it: *Calida Fornax*—hot oven.

He topped a rise, spurring the lineback on a hunch. He turned in the saddle, watched his backtrail.

That's when he knew.

His hunch had paid off.

Someone was back there. He had seen the top of a hat. Someone ducking, just as the dun cleared the rise. Someone who didn't want to be seen.

Buck cursed, looked around him at the desolate land. There were few places to hide.

No law against anyone following him, but why did that someone duck when he knew he might be seen? Who was it? Someone he knew? Someone who had trailed him from Prescott? Knew his destination?

He wanted to make the springs before the sun hit him full in the face, yet he didn't want to push his horse. That could be fatal to both of them. A man without a horse in this country was just as bad off as a man without water.

If someone had trailed him from Prescott, it hadn't been easy. He had ridden mostly at night, across the Colorado and over the Mojave.

He held up below the rise, waited.

23

The Winchester in its scabbard was warm, but not too hot to touch. He jerked it loose, so it would be ready if he needed it.

He held the horse there in the shallow ravine, listening. A light breeze jostled the joshua trees, rattled the yuccas. The sweat on his back turned suddenly chill and he shivered at the sudden change. His eyes scanned the dim windblown trail. He looked up at the sheer rock faces of the Monuments, hazy and low on the horizon.

He waited a long time, until he was as nervous as the horse.

No one came.

Buck clucked to the lineback, jogged him gently with his spurs.

The trail widened, the land changed.

Buck circled, once, found no signs of anyone following him.

Had he imagined it then? The desert could play tricks on a man. The high desert, with its clear, thin air, could do the same.

He rode into country that had low hillocks and shallow gullies where a man couldn't see ahead more than a few hundred yards.

The deeper into this eerie silent land, the more apprehensive he became. Now, there was almost too much to see. The joshuas all looked like men, standing there, stalking him. The lineback dun spooked at every bend of the trail.

Then, he heard something. Or thought he did. A sound or a feeling, he wasn't sure which. Maybe both. A click of a shod hoof on stone, an iron shoe sliding through sand. Something. He hauled in the reins, listening hard.

The sound of his breathing was loud. Far off, a high hawk wheeled, hunting movement below. A quail's trilled alarm sounded over a hill.

Buck was in a gully, cut off from sight of the high ground. He didn't like it much. He worried the unlit cigar in his mouth, jogged the horse to move out of the gully.

By then, it was too late.

They were waiting for him at the top of the shallow rim.

He counted three men, at first. Then, another, four hundred yards off, sitting his horse, watching.

The men had rifles aimed straight at him.

"Hold up there," said one of them.

Buck reined in. He thought about going for it, but they had him braced. Three .44-40 Winchesters leveled at his chest.

His hazel eyes scanned the men quickly. One was lean, with curly yellow hair and thin lips. His cowmen's clothes had seen some wear. He looked to be about twenty-four, twenty-five or so. Another wore the trappings of a Californio: wide-brimmed Spanish hat, flared pants and sash, big-roweled Spanish spurs. He was dark-haired, heavy in the torso. He wasn't a Mexican. The third wore yellow pants and a red shirt, dark hat shadowing his face. He spat tobacco through brown, jagged teeth.

The fourth man was too far away to make out. He just sat there, as if he was under a cloud shadow, although he was actually in the open,

25

near a joshua tree.

"What's the worry?" asked Buck evenly.

"Just light down and don't make no quick moves," said the Californio.

Buck lifted up easily off the saddle and swung down. He touched the ground easy, his hands in full view, away from his gun belt.

"Just don't do nothing but stand real still," said the man in the red shirt. This one dismounted and led the lineback out of the way. He patted the saddle bags, and the rifle in its scabbard.

"Throw out your pistol," said the young man with light hair. "Take it out butt first and just toss it out in front of you about ten paces."

Buck did as he was told.

Yellow Hair slid from the saddle, his rifle never leaving its aiming point. He walked to the pistol. Something he was carrying jingled as if he had a pocket full of loose coins. It was an odd sound that Buck noted. The man picked up Buck's pistol and tucked it into his belt.

"That'll be it for this *pistolero,*" said the Californio. "You can just say your prayers, feller. You got time. You're gonna die real slow," he told Buck.

"He'll never see Belleville, that's for sure," said Red Shirt.

"Shut up," said the Californio.

Buck's eyes narrowed.

"You got any good reason to kill me? You want my horse, my guns? Take them."

No one answered him. Yellow Hair remounted, untied the thongs from his lariat. He shook out a loop.

"You ain't got no say about it, feller," he said.

Buck saw the rope whirling, made a run for it. He heard the whistle-whisper of the loop. It settled perfectly around him. He tried to throw up his arms, but he was too late. The loop, like a snare trap, drew in around his chest. He heard the horse back up as the rope tautened. His legs went out from under him. There was only air between him and the ground.

He hit hard, felt the rope jerk tight around his chest.

"Give him a ride," said Red Shirt. "Tear some skin."

Yellow Hair said nothing. His horse worked the rope, stretching it like a good cow pony, sliding backwards, keeping it taut.

Buck knew enough not to struggle. He was hooked like a trout and that horse would keep backing up as long as there was slack. He brought his hands up, grabbed the loop and held on.

He knew the kid was going to drag him.

Yellow Hair did just that.

He put spurs to his mount and reined the horse to a path. A hard path. Through brush and cactus, over rocks and sand, angling to swing Buck into joshuas and Spanish bayonets.

Buck screamed in pain as sharp stones gouged his body, whacked hard against his shoulder blades. He winced as cactus spines pierced his skin. He glanced off nopal and skimmed through cholla with delicate screaming needles. He slammed into joshuas, broke yuccas in half, bounced off half-buried boulders.

His flesh turned to pulp. Pain dug into his senses like knives, hollowed out nerve ends until they shrieked. He twisted, dodged, as best he could, but the rider jerked him until he was nearly senseless.

Somewhere, far off, he heard the crack of rifle fire. The sun spun dizzily in the sky.

He skidded to a stop, still conscious.

The rope was slack.

He turned over, groaned.

Yellow Hair hissed at him, a knife in his hands. He had cut the rope.

More shots sounded.

Buck struggled to a sitting position.

The youth drew a pistol, took aim.

"I reckon we'll just have to finish you off early," he said.

Buck rolled.

The pistol boomed with a shattering explosion. Buck kept rolling, the pain blinding him until he wanted to scream. He heard the crack-spang of the lead as it caromed off a stone where his head had been.

Red Shirt came riding by, shouting.

"Come on, boy, we got troubles. If he lives, we'll kill him some other time."

He had Buck's horse in tow and was slapping his own horse's flanks with the tail ends of his reins.

The Californio rode by as if whipped by the devil. He leaned over the pommel of his saddle, raked spurs against his horse's flanks.

Buck tried to stand, half-fell, in agony. He watched them go, heading toward the mountains, his own destination.

They all followed the fourth man, the one who stayed so far off he could not be recognized. Who was he? Someone Buck knew? It was a puzzle. The whole incident was a puzzle.

He tried to stand, felt a wetness on his back. Sticky, like blood.

The pain made him falter, fall.

Someone must hate him a hell of a lot to do such a thing.

Buck shaded his eyes, peered up at the sun.

A man could die out here, he thought.

But someone had saved him. Who? Good shots. Good enough to drive off the men who had braced him.

He lurched toward a piece of shade, narrow as a toothpick.

He was bleeding, but he was alive.

Somewhere, in the back of his mind, was a thought.

He knew what it was. He had felt it before.

Hate.

CHAPTER TWO

Buck squinted, partly in pain, partly to shield his eyes from the blinding sun.

The men had gone, but he still imagined he saw them on the horizon where they had disappeared. They were headed in the direction he had been going. To Belleville. And they had known he was going there. How?

He grunted, tried to sit up. He heard something squish and wondered if his insides had been pounded to pulp. A sharp pain speared through his abdomen. A wave of dizziness assailed him and he fought to keep from falling over, burying his face in the hot sand.

He struggled to stand, knowing that if he stayed there any longer he might never get up. He gained his feet, swayed unsteadily. The pain flooded his body, grated against his teeth. Knives scored his flesh, dug into the nerves. He gritted his teeth, took a faltering step toward the meagre shade of a joshua tree. He found some small cigars in his shirt pocket, put one between his teeth. That would help keep his mouth from drying out. The tobacco tasted foul.

All through his agony, a single thought kept yammering at him, like a bird in the woods you can never see, calling insistently, over and over, with the same raucous notes. *Whoever those men where, they had known he was coming.*

They had known he was coming and they'd taken him without a fight. They had to have been trailing him, watching him a long time before he got to that spot. It was a good spot to take a man because it was a high spot between two low ones. But who were they? And why had they wanted to make him die slow? Dragging a man through hot sands, over rock and brush smacked of revenge. Yet he had never laid eyes on any of them before.

He thought of the fourth man. Why had he stayed off from the others, afraid to show himself? Maybe he was someone Buck knew. From somewhere else. From another time.

He left the tiny shade, knowing he had to go on. To Belleville. Would they be waiting for him? Sometimes a man could walk down another on horseback. But he was out here with no gun and no water. Maybe they thought he wouldn't make it. Someone had sure as hell chased them away. Someone they were afraid of enough to leave him and ride on. Maybe they thought he would die out here anyway. He might, too. It was a grim thought, but was soon replaced by an even keener one.

The one man, the one who dressed like a Californio, but was a gringo, had called him a *pistolero*. The name rang a bell in Buck's head.

31

He hadn't heard that term in a long time. Not since Texas. But who had called him that? His mind clouded with the vapors of thoughts and he didn't know the answer. It was a long walk to water and the sun was rising higher and higher in the blue sky.

He staggered on, trying to fight down the pain. He slapped the flies that boiled over the lacerations on his shoulder. The sun seared the raw flesh, dried the blood into temporary scabs.

Another thing bothered Buck. The man had mentioned Belleville. How did they know he was headed there? Had he said something back in Prescott? He might have. Probably did. He thought he had told Billy or Turk that this was where he was headed. They had checked him over when he rode in with the horses and mules to sell. They had become friends because the brands checked out. Those weren't "two-way" animals. He had bought them in Los Angeles, sold them at profit in Arizona.

But he didn't remember seeing any of these men there. Maybe the fourth man. That had to be it. He had been in Prescott, at the saloon. He had overheard Buck telling those two bounty men about his plans.

If so, then Buck had probably seen him and . . . or was it, just maybe, someone he knew? A friend who was not a friend anymore?

It was puzzling and it occupied Buck's mind until his throat went dry, despite the cigar he worried in his mouth. His sweat soaked him cool at first, then left him hot as it dried up and the moisture in his body would not come through the pores of his skin anymore.

Ahead, Buck could see no signs of life and he soon lost track of how long he had been walking. The sun was now in front of him, burning through his clothes, parching his throat. He had chewed the cigar down to a stub. He didn't see any barrel cactus and the *nopales* were withered by months of dry weather and blazing sun. But he kept heading west the way the sun was headed. He knew, though, after a while, that if he didn't find water, he was liable to die.

He scanned the empty land with hazel eyes, searched for a sign of water, leafy trees, rocks where a spring might be, a dry river bed where he could dig down under the sand and find moisture.

The land was dry, bleak.

His hatred for the four men burned still hotter, hot as the afternoon sun.

The morning wore on into afternoon. An afternoon of relentless heat, boiling sands stretched interminably into the hottest part of the day. Buck's boot soles were so hot they burned through his socks, scorched his feet. Once, he fell and only the searing sands brought him to his feet again. He was badly dehydrated, dangerously giddy.

Buck knew he couldn't last long.

His body cried out for moisture. His tongue swelled in his mouth, felt like an alien plum. A lesser man would have succumbed to the desert heat hours ago. Buck kept on going, something in him refusing to surrender his spirit and his flesh to the sun, the sand, or the buzzards. But he was no longer able to know whether he was walking four miles an hour or two. Or only one. Nor did he any longer know for sure if he was traveling in the right direction. His feet were leaden weights moving through thick arid mud. The landscape danced around him like a shimmering mirror on a teetering table. Heat waves rose up from every sandhill, every stone until he felt suffocated, like a claustrophobe in a prison cell. Lakes rose up from the desert floor and retreated as he plodded near, tantalizing, maddening mirages that drained away as if dammed over an invisible sinkhole far beneath the surface.

He began to talk to himself, rationally at first, then idiotically with the words making no sense to him, only babble that came from far away, from someone other than himself. He saw men on the horizon, waved to them, stumbled toward them, only to see them disappear like smoke, like magic lantern images on a wall when the flame sputters out. He heard thundering hoofbeats in his ears. He turned, looked wildly around, expecting to see buffalo or horsemen, but saw only emptiness and sunlight bouncing off quartz veins in the rocks. His eyes burned in their sockets, became raw and sensitive as if fine sand had been sprinkled in the mucous-lined pouches, as if they had been sprinkled with fine ground pepper and rubbed dry.

As the sun started to descend toward the ocean beyond the desert and the mountains, he thought it must be a hell waiting for him over the next rise. He stared it straight in the face and felt as if someone was beating him with heated blankets. He walked through a furnace and no longer felt the pain in his numbed feet. They were like clubs, awkward, useless appendages that had no toes or heels or soles. Just things that kept him upright, kept him going when he no longer could find a reason to go on.

He saw his mother and father with a picnic basket waving to him from the cool shade of a green tree by a sparkling stream. He saw a waterfall behind them, cascading down mossy green rocks, splashing into a deep pool. He hollered and the odd husk that came from his throat was not his own voice, but the awful wrenching sound of a wounded animal bleating its last breath.

"I'm coming!" he yelled, but it sounded like a hoarse scream.

He started to run, stumbled. He fell into a spiny nopal and thought he had fallen into an ant hill. He rose to his feet, brushed off the thousands of tiny red ants crawling over his clothes. He screamed again and when he looked for his parents, they were gone—and so was the green tree and the stream, the bridal veil waterfall and the deep cool pool.

He wept then, sobbed without any tears until his throat throbbed and he coughed up dry dust and blood.

He cursed in every language he knew and made up words when he could no longer think of any. And the words made sense to him and he knew he was going mad because a day had gone by and the sun was at his back and he had been cool for a time, sleeping half-dead on sands that held the heat all night long. Time had slipped away from him, emptied him out, left him a shell scuttling across the endless hell toward a place that had ceased to exist. His tongue was a swollen knob in his mouth. His lips had cracked and bled and were now desiccated, without any sensation.

He had lost a day and he kept seeing towns and water holes and people coming and going.

And then he saw horses and expected them to drift away, but they stayed there, and they got bigger and bigger as he staggered toward them. He saw men, too, but they were lying motionless, their limbs twisted and swollen until the pants seemed so tight they would burst and their shirts strangled their swollen arms and backs. A stench rose from the land and he saw the buzzards flap and amble awkwardly over to a corpse and bob its hideous head down, its beak tearing into gamy flesh.

Buck felt the bile stir in his gut, but there was no fluid in his stomach and he wretched until his eyes bulged from their sockets.

There were two men. Dead.

He forced himself to look at their faces.

One of them he knew. Turk Reeve. His face was black, ballooned almost beyond recognition. The other was a stranger, bloated into his clothes. His eyes were gone, pecked out by the buzzards.

"Jesus," said Buck and staggered away from the stench, from the grim reminders of his own mortality.

He went thirty yards and mercifully passed out. The ground rose up to him but he had no strength to stop it. He didn't put out his arms. He fell with a jarring thud and lights danced in his brain until it was pitch dark and he no longer felt anything.

CHAPTER THREE

The two men approached the scene of death warily.

They had been here before.

Weary, they circled the site.

"Looks like they's an extry one here," said Nick. "Jess Buck made it after all."

"That's Jess Buck?"

"Less I miss my guess. Done for, I reckon."

"He ain't movin'," said Nick Tanner, his voice hollow, reedy. There was fear in his voice, an awestruck quality as he surveyed the bloated dead men, the body of a man for whom he held much respect.

"Better do some clean up and buryin'," said Billy Edwards quietly. "You fetch up them horses."

"Thanks," said Nick, glad to get away from the smell and the sight of the men he had ridden with only yesterday. He rode off toward Turk's horse. The other man's mount, a blue roan, was tangled in chaparral and sage, a half mile away. The man was a rancher who had raised horses, had them rustled. His name was Ben Kirley.

"Hey Nick, you come on back here. Quick."

Nick Tanner turned in the saddle, saw Billy bending over Buck's body.

"He alive?" he asked, without hope.

"Barely. Bring that canteen."

Nick rode over, hefted the canteen from the saddle horn. They were only two miles from Twentynine Palms. The canteen was full. The young man galloped his horse to where Billy now cradled Buck in his arms. Nick's straw hair stuck out from under a dusty felt hat. He was a short, stocky lad, with pale brown eyes, a snaggle-toothed grin, freckles sprinkled over his face. He leaned over, handed the canteen to Billy Edwards.

Billy pulled the cork out of the wooden canteen with his teeth, forced a trickle of water over Buck's parched lips. Buck didn't stir. His mouth, open, slack, dribbled water onto his sand-clogged chest.

Nick swung down from his horse, ground-tied the sorrel to a good-sized stone.

"Is he — will he make it?" he asked Billy.

Edwards shook his head. He was a man in his late thirties, with a small, weathered face, pinched by years of being in all kinds of hard weather. His lips were as lined as his hands with age marks. Billy was tall, lanky, thin from those same years of hard living in the outdoors. He was tough as a boot, with colorless blue eyes that seemed almost grey.

"He's plumb parched. Looks like they took a

rope to him, dragged him."

Nick looked at Buck's torn clothes, the bruises and scratches on exposed flesh. He winced.

"They was doin' that to him when we jumped 'em?"

"I reckon," said Billy. He poured more water on Buck's lips. He leaned over, put an ear against the unconscious man's chest, the left side. He listened for several seconds. "Heart's working straight. Bet his blood's thick as goat's milk."

"Jess Buck . . . he—he sure has changed some."

"You 'member him?"

"I was in short britches when he killed those men at my pa's place. Never thought I'd see him up close. He's bigger'n you are, Billy."

"He's tall, all right. Solid. Nothin' broke. Bastids left him thout water or horse. Kilt Turk and Kirley."

"You reckon they's the ones we were after?"

"Dunno. They was in Prescott. Seemed mighty interested in Buck. First I thought Buck was in with 'em."

"You know different now?"

"Well, he ain't with 'em anymore." Billy pried open Buck's lips, poured in a mouthful of water. He closed the lips, tilted the man back. Buck choked, swallowed. His eyes fluttered open, stared at the sky without focusing. Billy poured water over his face, shook him gently.

"Wake up, Buck."

Buck gasped, shuddered. He tried to sit up. Billy poured more water on his lips. His eyes opened again, focused on Billy.

"More," he rasped.

"Too much right now and you won't make it, pard," said Edwards. "Easy does it."

Buck took a deep breath and looked at his benefactor.

"Thanks," he husked, his voice like the crackle of dried corn leaves.

"Can you make it to your feet, Buck? We'll tote you into some shade."

Buck nodded. Nick and Billy helped him to his feet. He swayed uncertainly. Billy got an arm under his, took his weight on his own shoulders.

"Get that blue roan over here, Nick. We can ride to the Palms where there's shade, water."

"Water," rasped Buck.

Nick reached down for the canteen, gave it to Billy.

"Don't swaller more'n a mouthful," warned Billy. "Let it trickle down slow so's your stomach gets used to it."

Buck nodded, opened his mouth desperately.

Nick caught up his horse, rode after the blue roan. A few minutes later, they got Buck mounted. Nick led Turk's horse, while Billy made sure Buck stayed in the saddle on the roan. A half hour later, they sat in shade, next to a watering trough.

Buck sipped water slowly for an hour. He climbed into the trough, soaked there in the cool.

"You the one run those men off?" he asked Billy.

"Cost two lives. Ben Kirley, who hired us out,

and Turk. Turk was a good man."

"Know who they were?"

Billy shook his head.

"You rode out of Prescott, they was right behind you. We was right behind them."

Buck looked at Nick. There was something familiar about him. But he didn't think he'd ever seen him before. He stared at the youth a long time. Nick grinned, offered him the makings. Buck shook his head.

"I know you from somewhere?"

"I'm Nick Tanner."

"Tanner. . . . Texas?"

"Been a long time."

"A long time, Mister Buck."

"You riding with Billy?"

"I worked for Ben Kirley. He raised Morgans, started mixing 'em with Arabs. Has a ranch over in Apple Valley, this side of Victor. The B bar K."

"Don't know it," said Jess. "I recollect a Kirley back in Texas. Outside of Monihans. Tryin' to remember the brand. Lazy K, I think."

"That was Ben's brother, Jean. Ben came out here four years ago. I been with him nigh on two year."

Buck pulled out a soggy cigar from his pocket. He broke it in half, stuck one half in his mouth. He was still sick, woozy. His skin felt like it was on fire. There were lumps and bruises on him; tender spots that felt mushy when he touched them.

He got out of the trough, walked gingerly into the shade of a palm tree.

"Never expected to see you again Billy. Why didn't you tell me you and Turk were headed this way. I'd have rode with you."

Billy allowed himself a faint smile.

"Couldn't then. You get a good look at the men who dragged you, stole your horse?"

"Three of them. One of 'em stayed off. Like he was running things."

"I only made three. A kid they call Jingles, is the only name I have."

"Mind telling me what this is all about?"

Billy and Nick exchanged looks.

"This Jingles is a spotter," said Billy. "He rides alone, takes up at a horse ranch. Next thing you know some stock turns up missing. He's always alibied. But, he leaves, goes somewhere else. First time I seen him in Prescott and he was with two other men. The one in the Californio outfit and his partner. Now I can't prove nothing, but I figure I got something. Nick and Ben have just lost twenty head of Arab-Morgan horses and two men sold thirty head with two different brands.

"One brand is a Box B Bar H. Now that's B bar K, less I miss my guess. Other'ns a Lazy H. Once a Lazy K. Both them brands run on Kirley's range and I got to tell Jean I buried his brother and the men who rustled their stock has got away clean. You tell me about that fourth man. He shoots real good with a sporting rifle. Me and Nick about bought it. We get past the Palms here and their tracks fade like smoke. Real slick outfit."

Buck let out a low whistle.

"What'd they jump me for?" he asked.

Billy shrugged.

"They looked you over pretty good in Prescott. I started to figure you for one of 'em. Up until yesterday. They sure as hell left you to die and either you crossed them or they had your number on a bullet. I reckon when someone drags a man, he's got a real big grudge."

"I never saw any of them before."

"They meant to kill you, but in case they didn't, they took all you had and left you to die out there. You should have died."

"Well, I'm glad you two boys come along," said Buck soberly.

"Damned lucky," said Billy. "Another twenty minutes in that sun and you'd have been buzzard bait for sure."

Buck jammed his hand in his pocket. He was almost dry now. He felt the smooth leather pouch. At least those horse thieves hadn't taken his pocket gold.

"I need a horse and gun," said Buck. "I can pay for 'em."

Nick got up, grinning.

"I can sell you Ben's roan. I don't think Jean would mind."

"I've got a spare pistol in my kit," said Billy. "It's yours."

"I'll pay," said Buck.

Billy waved his offer away. He walked to his horse, got out an oilcloth. He unwrapped the Colt .45. The bluing was worn off the barrel, but it had good butt stocks of rosewood.

"This'll fill that empty holster of your'n," said

Billy, handing the pistol to him. "I've got a box of ca'tridges for it, too."

Nick emptied Ben's saddlebags, brought the roan over.

"I reckon fifty for the horse and saddle," he said.

Buck looked the horse over. It was sound of limb, had a good chest. The brand was B bar K.

"I'll give you a hundred. You buy Billy here a steak for his pistol. I'll need a bill of sale."

"I got a canteen for you, too, Jess," said Nick. "I owe you. You saved my pa's life."

"At least I know I haven't got one of those one-way horses," said Buck. "I'm mighty obliged to you two."

"I wouldn't go on to Belleville, was I you," said Billy. "You might not be so lucky next time."

"How'd you know I was going there?"

"Hell," said Billy, "in Prescott when you was in your cups that's all you talked about."

Buck grinned sheepishly.

They ate beans and salt pork. Buck slept deep. When he awoke in the morning, Billy and Nick were gone. They had left him a small sack of hardtack, some pork and dried beans, four handfuls of coffee and two empty cans for cooking.

He thanked them silently and rode off, stiff from sleeping on the ground, ragged and sore from being dragged, but full of fresh spring water. The blue roan was frisky for five minutes and then settled down.

Buck headed for Belleville, six bullets in the

chamber of the Colt, a full box of shells in his saddlebags. He tapped his pocket where the gold pouch lay. He felt rich, glad to be alive.

Five miles from Twentynine Palms he saw the tracks of Billy and Nick veer off the trail, cut south. He had heard there were hot springs down that way and that it was easier. But he kept on west and before he reached Yucca Valley, he picked up the tracks of the men he sought.

Five horses.

Four ridden, one led.

CHAPTER FOUR

Buck tracked the four ambushers long enough to know where they were headed. They had tried to hide their tracks, but he tumbled to their methods after a couple of hours. The men would split up, drag brush, meet again. They rode the dry washes, the stream beds.

He followed the tracks along the dim trail until it was too dark to see, then made camp near a pile of boulders on high ground. He stayed well away from the fire, never looked at it directly. Coyotes howled and yapped. He heated enough water for one cup of coffee, chewed on a chunk of warmed pork. He looked at the land around him, full of shadows and moonlit shapes. The joshuas looked like men surrounding him, arms outstretched. The stars overhead seemed close enough to touch and he wondered at them as he had so many times before.

Buck slept long and well. He was up early, still hurting from being dragged through the brush and burned by the sun. But the sleep had helped hurry the healing process and he was fit enough to grumble when he realized he had chewed up his last cigar the night before.

A single cup of coffee and hardtack chewed slowly was his way of breaking his fast. He cleaned up his camp, moved out in the predawn light, grateful for the miles he would ride in the cool before the sun beat down on him again. When it was light enough to see, he saw the wide swatch of hoof prints. The ambushers were moving fast and they had not stopped long in any one place. He found a night camp, saw that they posted a man as guard, but only three of them stood watch. The fourth man, he reasoned, apparently gave the orders.

The trail cut west of the town settled by Mormons, once part of El Rancho San Bernardino. The land grew steeper, rockier. He began to see a prospector's hut or two and he stopped at one to water the roan, late in the afternoon. At first, he thought it was deserted, but a man in his fifties came to the door of the clapboard shack, a double-barreled Greener in his hand.

"Howdy," said Buck. "Wondered where I was and if you could spare water for my horse?"

"You be on the Old Woman Springs Trail, east of Deadman's Point if you're going up the Valley, and I haul my water from Stoddard's Wells."

Buck saw the mules in a pine-pole corral out back.

"He won't drink more'n a hatful."

"Set down, then, stranger."

The old man put down his Greener, led Buck around back to a wooden tank set in the rocks for shade. Buck let the roan drink.

The prospector studied the brand on the horse's rump.

"It's not a one-way horse," said Buck. "It's paid for."

"You one of them Mormons?"

"Nope."

"Figured not. You heading for Victor."

"Bear Valley. Belleville."

"Looks like you tangled with a mess of wildcats. Or wolves."

Buck laughed.

"You see four men ride through here? Late yesterday?"

Maybe, maybe not. Who's asking."

"Jess Buck. Those were my wolves."

The prospector cracked a toothless grin. He was stooped, haired over with a long greying beard, balding under his battered hat. He said his name was Corny Poole. He pointed to the mountains as Buck pulled the roan's head out of the water. The horse snorted and blew, shook out its mane.

"Came here in Sixty," said Poole, "and worked them mountains like a Trojan. Through the war until the gold petered out and Lucky Baldwin closed his mine. But, there's wealth up there yet. Not for the likes of you, but for a man what thinks of the future and can wait patient. Mother lode was never found and some still make a living up in the Holcomb Valley. But they's too many hardcases there now and I stay down here on the high desert."

"There's gold down here?"

Corney's eyes narrowed in suspicion.

"They's minerals all about."

"I'm not after gold."

"No, but you're after something, feller, and you wear that sidearm like a man who don't use it for no hammer."

"I heard there was snakes out here."

"Mojave greens and you step around 'em. One bites your horse and he's got less'n an hour to live. One bites you and you got about twenty minutes."

"Never heard of 'em."

"Rattlers. Mean as sin."

Buck mounted up.

"Poole, thanks for the water."

"Ain't got any whiskey have you?"

"None. Nor tobacco."

"You don't have much."

"No. If you saw those men and they were leading a horse, the horse was mine."

"I saw 'em and they was in a powerful hurry. I seed 'em before."

"They got names?"

Poole shook his head.

"Not any they was born with, I reckon. You'll find 'em up in Holcomb Valley. Belleville."

Buck tipped his hat, rode away from the hut. He looked back once, but the old man was gone.

The mountains grew closer, bigger, but he knew he was still a long way off. The air was clear and everything looked closer. He rode until sunset, following the tracks of the men who had robbed him. The road widened and other tracks joined those of the men he sought. He took the road that cut to the mountains. He looked for the Army post, but trees blocked his view. He found some rocks to give him protection and made his camp there. He made no fire. It could have been easily seen for miles and he did not know if the bushwackers had left a man behind to watch their back trail.

The trees meant water, and the next morning he followed the trail cutting through the mountains. The road was now rutted with wagon tracks and he spoke to men at Whiskey Springs who were polite but tightlipped. He asked no questions, gave no information. They rode mules and they didn't smile much.

He rode into the high country where pinon trees appeared suddenly and pines, cedars. The air was scented with them and when he looked back, he saw the plain spread out like a vast quilt. The roan climbed the steep road well and they made the crest before noon. At a small lake, the trail parted and he did not know which way to ride. There were so many tracks he could not separate those he wanted to see out of the others. He took the rough road that wound around the mountain and the lake.

There were houses and false front buildings on a flat. He stopped a man and asked where he was.

"Starvation Flat."

"I'm looking to go to Belleville."

"Up the Van Duzen road there. Just follow it."

"This is Bear Valley?"

"It is. You goin' to the hanging?"

"No. Where is that?"

"Belleville. Where most ever'body is. You got time to make it. I'm just now going to get a buggy for the wife and chilluns."

Buck rode on up the Van Duzen trail, passing wagons and riders all heading the same direction. He followed the stream of people. His blood quickened when he saw a sign that said *Belleville*. He tapped the Colt, loosened it in its holster.

Then he saw where the crowd had gathered and his stomach twisted up.

At the juncture of several roads, beyond the edge of town, people gaped at a huge, double—trunked juniper tree. Four ropes dangled from a large branch. Buck felt his horse jostled along. He drifted to the edge of the road, scanned every face, looking for the men he sought. At first, he thought the hanging might be for them.

Four men stood lined up under the juniper tree, nooses dangling above their heads.

He could not see their faces.

As he strained to see, four horses were brought up and the men, their hands bound behind their backs, lifted into the saddles. Other men fitted the nooses around their necks. Buck wanted to yell at them, tell them to wait, but he didn't want to call attention to himself. He saw one man ride up to the men, check the knots, snug them up tight under their ears. He shuddered. He clapped his heels to the roan's flanks.

Buck stood up in the stirrups, trying to see the faces and clothes of the men waiting to be hanged. Before he could get close, there was a pistol shot and the four horses bolted, leaving their riders jerking in the air, twitching in their death throes.

As he rode closer, the men at the end of the ropes gradually stopped kicking. A murmur rippled through the crowd of spectators. Buck scanned their faces, looking for the men who left him to die in the desert. The hanged men turned slowly in the afternoon sun, their boot toes pointed down, their necks broken, heads tilted sideways as if sleeping.

Someone tacked a sign to the hanging tree. People stood on tiptoe, craned their necks to see what the sign said. Buck circled the crowd, trying to see the faces of the four dead men.

Eyes narrowed, hat brim pulled low over his eyes, Buck moved around the perimeter of the throng.

Some of the people began to drift away. Some glanced up at him, then turned away as if they had been caught at something shameful. A few of the men passed bottles and made jokes. A woman frowned at them and turned away, hiking up her skirts to keep from tripping. Someone walked out onto the meadow and vomited loudly. He heard someone sobbing softly.

"Cut 'em down," hollered a man at the edge of the crowd.

"Leave 'em strung up," yelled another, with a differing viewpoint.

"As an example, yeah!" said a man, shaking his fist in the air.

53

"Let everybody see how we take care of no accounts!"

Buck swung out of the saddle, felt the stirrup take up his weight. The leather creaked as he held onto the saddle horn let himself down. He looked around him at the people streaming back to their homes or to the saloons. Decent looking folks mostly. Some miners with tired, sagging faces, their skin tanned to leather from the sun. Young boys in faded trousers and thin muslin shirts made gestures and faces to mime the looks on the faces of the hanged men as they died. He saw a few prosperous-looking men and a couple of girls who looked like they might be more at home in the dance hall.

He looked them over. The people who lived and worked in Belleville. The people who had just hanged four men.

Several people looked at him as he stopped in front of the juniper tree.

He ignored them, stared up at the faces of the men dangling from ropes wrapped around the juniper's sprawling limbs. His gaze shifted to the sign tacked to one of the trunks.

The sign was handpainted, the letters crude:

NOTICE

THIS IS WHAT OUTLAWS GET IN
BELLEVILLE.

THIS IS A GOOD TOWN.

WE AIM TO KEEP IT THAT WAY.

BEWARE!!!

Buck brought his hand up over his brows to shade his eyes from the rays of the falling afternoon sun.

He looked again at the faces of the hanged men.

He wanted to make damned sure.

He wanted to know if they were the ones he had been trailing for the past two days.

He wanted to know if Belleville had done his killing for him.

CHAPTER FIVE

A half dozen men rode up to the juniper tree. Another bunch came on foot. The men on horseback slashed the ropes with knives, cutting the dead men down. A wagon rumbled up to the tree. Buck watched as they loaded the corpses in like sacks of meal.

He looked long and hard at the dead men's faces, their features twisted out of alignment by suffocation. He had never laid eyes on any of them before.

But, they looked not much different from a lot of men he'd seen. Dead men. Dead did something to a man's face if he didn't die at peace with himself and the world. Violent death darkened the hollows of a man's eyes. Like these men.

Like those men in Tanner's saloon so long ago.

Buck could still see their twisted faces in his mind.

And other faces.

Like the first man Buck killed after he left Monihans.

Waco. He had gone there after that. He was

still just a kid, with a kid's face. But, he had a reputation and they called him a *pistolero*. The brand followed him and the reputation stuck to him. He had hired on with a cattle outfit, hoping to ride clear to Sedalia and leave his past behind.

In Waco, where the gather had been driven, he went into town with his foreman, Orville Watkins, and a couple of other boys to shake off dust gathered down in the barrancas and along the trail. Deep, embedded dust that no river would wash out of the throat.

The Tumbleweed Saloon was not much of a place. A long wooden bar made with rough lumber, tacked to barrels, some tables, crate chairs, a card room, no women. The owner had tried to make it liveable with deer heads, a buffalo cape spread on the big empty wall, pronghorn antelope antlers for hatracks. There were saw chips on the floor and brass goboons, pickled goose eggs and jerky in jars, peacock feathers stuck into a smoked cracked mirror, and oil lamps that blackened the walls with soot.

Jess Buck thought it was grand place. Very manly and private. He felt good about Orville asking him to join him for a drink. The other boys tired of it quick, but Watkins liked it because the whiskey was good and raw without too much hot pepper and tobacco in it. He was a raw-boned, rawhide man whose purple veins threaded a rosy face with jutting cheekbones and close-set eyes bracketing a bent nose that made wheezing noises when Orville breathed. He was not tall, but wide as a cornerstone for a Saint Louie building and his belly hung out over legs trim as a thoroughbred stallion. He was top-heavy, but he carried his excess weight with grace, and in the saddle, he was taller than most men. He knew cattle and he knew men.

"Better watch the jasper down the bar, Jess," he said. "Had his eyes on you for the last ten hunnert grains."

Buck glanced sideways down the bar, saw the man eyeing him. Orville knew the story of Tanner's, knew, like Buck, it had traveled over the trails, been spoke of around the campfires, in the saloons. Orville was fifty years old, but he looked forty when the sun was just right on him. He had been a piece and when he spoke a man listened careful.

"You still use a hourglass, Orv?"

"Used it enough to know time."

"I don't know the man."

"Your name's been mentioned enough in here. We can go over to the Waco, find some pretty girls."

"I like it here."

"Don't like it too much."

Orville drank his whiskey, turned to face Buck. Jess was between Watkins and the curious stranger.

Some seconds ticked by. Grains fell through an hourglass.

The stranger drank another swallow or two, kept looking down at Buck. There was no one between him and Jess. The bartender went into the back room. Crates rattled, shoes scuffed on dirt.

The men at the tables lowered their voices.

Buck felt a lead rod straighten his spine.

"You the *pistolero?*" called the stranger.

Every sound in the place got sucked into a hole.

It was dead quiet.

Jess turned slowly, faced the lean, hardbitten man at the far end of the bar.

"No," he said.

The lean man, swarthy-complexioned, pistol tied low on his leg, squared off, jutted a sharp chin in Buck's direction. He looked well put together, slightly casual after a couple of whiskies, relaxed enough to move fast, unafraid. Pushing. Pushing for something. A fight, a backdown. A point.

Buck felt like spitting in his face.

He, too, was warmed by whiskey. He was not drunk, but mellow as a November moon floating gold over the prairie. Felt good, as unafraid as jack-be-nimble.

"You know who I am?" asked the man.

"No."

"They call me Lobo. Ever hear of me?"

"No."

"You don't know much, do you sonny?"

"Not much," Buck admitted.

"Well, you gonna learn more. I heard about you. I think you got lucky. Why you ain't even dry behind the ears yet."

"I reckon not."

The man wanted to show off. Buck knew that. He also knew how close death was. He could hear

59

it whispering in his ear, could feel its light breath on his face. Like at Tanner's. He felt calm inside, but his blood ran hot. He had thought a lot, since then, about what had happened that day. It had been too easy to kill. He had been too quick with his gun. He didn't even remember drawing it, shooting it. Anger had blotted out reason. The man facing him now didn't know this, didn't know the dangerous current running inside Buck's skin. Like an electrified river. His flesh tingled, yet that deadly calmness settled over him like the quiet that comes before a terrible storm.

"Let's go, Jess," said Orv quietly. "The man's just trying to goad you."

Buck nodded. It was best to walk away.

He stepped away from the bar, not moving his hands. Orville plunked coin on the bar.

"We'll be leaving," he said, loudly.

"Not the kid," boomed Lobo. "The kid stays."

"I'm going too," said Buck, half-turned.

"No, by god!"

Lobo went into a crouch. His gun hand streaked for his holster.

It took just a moment, a flash of seconds, for Buck's gun to fill his hand. Lobo saw it and didn't believe it. His eyes went wide, and his gun hand slowed for just a fraction of time. But Buck's pistol came up fast and cocked. Buck didn't even aim, but pointed his barrel at Lobo like an extension of his finger.

The pistol boomed, belched smoke and flame, soft lead.

A smoking hole appeared on Lobo's chest as

his fingers closed around the butt of his own pistol.

Orville Reed cursed softly.

Dust puffed up from Lobo's vest. His knees buckled and his eyes glazed over with the frost of eternity.

"Jesus Christ," said a man.

"Fast," breathed another. "Faster'n lightning."

Buck felt a tug on his arm.

He stood there, his eyes hard as agates, smoke spooling out of the barrel of his pistol.

He turned, the quickness still in him, the flush of combat still suffusing his face.

"You'll likely have to remember this a long time," said Orville quietly. "There's men will hear about this and come after you."

"Why? He called me out."

"They want your reputation, Buck."

He had looked down at his smoking pistol, then, and frowned.

No, he didn't want it that way. But Orville had been right. They had come after him. Not because Lobo Esterhaus had any friends — he was a no-account, a troublemaker — but because they wanted to shoot down the man who had shot down Lobo.

Lobo had gone for his gun first. Everyone knew that. But that only made the story a better one to tell. The story got bigger and before long there was another town and a man riding in looking for Buck. He was a young man and they said he was tough. Buck had taken him down and had to ride on. He rode a long way, trying to live down a reputation he didn't want.

He'd been riding ever since and he'd seen a lot of dead men. Some were tallied on his sheet and some were like these four in Belleville — caught up in the dirty affairs of men and choked off from life by a rope or a bullet or a knife. It was still a lot for a man to think about, no matter how many he'd seen go down in death.

Buck walked his horse to the hitchrail in front of the Palace Hotel & Saloon.

He wrapped the reins around the smooth pine rail, hoping he would not be noticed for the stranger that he was.

Several men, however, made note of his arrival.

And, one woman.

Laurie Whiston, a willowy woman in her late twenties, drew a breath. Her breasts swelled against the tight bodice of her dress. She had stood on the porch, watched the man on the blue roan ride up to the hanged men and look them over. Now that she saw him up close, she turned away. Her eyes met those of her boss, Bert Singleton, the owner of the Palace. He, too, had been watching the stranger.

"Better get inside, Laurie," he said gruffly, "tend to your business."

"Bert, you have a way about you."

"Yes?"

"Even when you talk polite, you sound like you got a whip in your hand."

Singleton's eyes narrowed. The willow-slender woman with the auburn hair and green-blue eyes switched her skirts like a fan and went through the batwing doors of the hotel/saloon. Men crowded in for drinks behind her.

Singleton drew a cigar out of his vest pocket. He was a corpulent man, big in the shoulders, beefy around the middle. His face had puffed red when he saw the stranger stride up to the steps. He bit off the end of his cigar with a determined clench of teeth.

He knew a hunter when he saw one.

He wondered who the stranger was and what he was doing in Belleville.

Singleton nodded to a man on the far end of the porch.

Vern Slatter, a rangy tough with constantly flickering eyes, adjusted his low-slung, tied-down holster, loosened the pistol.

He followed Buck into the Palace.

Singleton lit his cigar, looked at the clumps of people still lingering along the street. The wagon with the dead men rumbled out of sight, headed for the undertaker's in San Bernardino.

His eyes caught sight of another man, narrowed.

Someone else was interested in the stranger.

Julio Machado returned Singleton's stare and a smile played over his lips.

Singleton fished a match out of his vest pocket, struck it on a porch post. He lit his cigar, blew a cloud of smoke out into the air. He flapped his coat back over the small pistol stuck in his waistband, tossed the burned-out match into the street.

He turned away from Machado's staring dark

eyes and went inside the Palace.

There were things he had to know about the stranger.

He had to know before anyone else.

He had to know now.

CHAPTER SIX

There were others, too, who saw Jess Buck come into Belleville.

Ted "Lucky" Foster was one of the biggest mine owners in Holcomb Valley. His two mines, the Lucky I and the Lucky II were still going full steam, producing high grade ore on the opposite slope where Baldwin's mine had flourished until the late sixties.

The gold fever was still high in Holcomb and Lucky's success attracted men who came to get their share and get out. Others, attracted by the gold, at first, and coming to love the mountains, stayed, gold or no gold.

Foster was one who had seen other potential in the high valley and, although he'd made his big stake from mining, was always on the lookout for other opportunities when the gold played out. It was his luck to find an untapped vein, but veins had a way of running out and, despite the talk rampant in Belleville about a "mother lode", he knew it was unlikely that any find would last long. The gold was there, he knew, but it was deep and secret, hard to dig out.

Lucky was a tall, wiry-tough man with hazel eyes flecked gold and green. He had a prophet's gaze and a wariness in his gaze born of hard dealings with men harder than he. His clothes, on this day, were tailored, expensive, showed their Los Angeles tailor's fineness of craft. The coat, vest, superbly cut trousers also showed that Lucky's ambition was strong; showed him to be a man who wanted to climb to a pinnacle in life and be respected.

It was true.

Lucky Foster wanted the best of everything, now that he had the means to get the best. But he didn't want riches and comfort for himself alone. His daughter, Amy, was the pride of his life. Nothing was too good for her.

Amy Foster lived on the Foster Ranch, even though she was of age, and every man who ever saw her had dreams about her forever afterward. Foster's spread adjoined the Holcomb's place and sprawled over a great deal of land beyond the diggings in and around Belleville.

Julio Machado helped Amy up into the Springfield buggy. Lucky nodded to him.

"You stayin' in town, Julio?"

Julio's eyes flickered.

"That man, the stranger, know him?"

Julio shrugged.

"Stay out of trouble." Lucky snapped the reins, the dark bay took up the slack in the traces, moved ahead. Foster nodded to several people. Amy tightened her bonnet's ribbon under her chin.

She looked back.

"Julio's going into the Palace," she said.

"I know," said her father.

"Do you know the man?"

"What man?"

"That man you and Julio were watching. I saw you. Both of you. Who is he?"

"I have no idea," said Foster.

But she detected the tension in his voice, the tautness in his throat.

And, she, too, wondered who the stranger was and why he had come to Belleville on that day.

Julio was a good foreman. He ran Foster's ranch for him, made sure that Lucky was not troubled with problems. His face was like a mask as he strode toward the Palace. His skin was brown as boot leather, with a touch of wine in it; his dark eyes like an eagle's, never missing much that was important. His high cheek bones bespoke his Indian blood and his town clothes were dark with white piping, cut in Californio style, the trousers bottoms flared like bells, tight-fitting. His pistol bore pearl handles and his ornate belt was studded with silver buttons. His black, flat-crowned hat, was wide-brimmed, tasseled.

He went through the bat-wings, drifted through the hotel lobby to the bar.

His eyes sought the stranger while his face bore no expression whatsoever.

The Palace was both elaborately decorated and gawdily cheap in its furnishings. Clapboard outside, but San Francisco fortyniner plush inside, with flocked red wallpaper, gilded moldings, expensive mirrors, glittery chandeliers. It looked like a bawdy house, but it was just a boomtown relic that had seen better days. The dancefloor catered to those men who sought female companionship, but the cribs above the saloon had been converted to offices and sleeping rooms where no man was allowed except Singleton or his employees. Of course the hotel could accommodate liasons between a man and a woman, but the letter of the law was followed.

Buck checked into the hotel first, was asked to pay in advance.

"Three dollars a night."

"Three dollars? For a bed?"

"You can sleep over to Sadie's for a dollar and a half."

"What's Sadie's?"

"Boarding house. One meal a day, coffee at breakfast. Breakfast is two bits."

Buck paid for one night. He had been in some towns where a bowl of mush and a milk cost a man ten dollars and a bed was twice that. He signed the register, went pstairs. So, he missed seeing Machado come through the lobby and he didn't know that other curious people were waiting for him to show up in the saloon.

The room was small, efficient. A bed, table, chairs, mirror, wash basin and pitcher. The window gave him a view of the meadow, the rocky hills at the edges, some of the placer diggings. He heard an *arrastre* groan as a mule turned the gears in its circling pace. Picks rang on stone from somewhere out of his vision and he heard laughter from a room down the hall. He washed up, vowed to buy a razor and lathering soap before morning.

The saloon continued to fill with spectators to the hanging as Buck made his way to the long bar. He saw men fix their gazes on him and put it down to curiosity. He wondered if the four men he was looking for were strangers here or if they were known.

He ordered a whiskey, avoided showing the curiosity that others showed toward him. He boxed his drink with his elbows on the bar, his hands outstretched. One boot rested on the brass footrail, the other nested in the fine saw shavings.

In the far corner of the room, Bert Singleton nodded to Laurie Whiston, then nodded again at the stranger.

Laurie arose from her chair and threaded her way to the bar. She sidled up to Buck.

He heard the rustle of cloth, smelled the faint cloying aroma of perfume.

"Hello, there," said Laurie.

He turned, looked into her clear blue eyes, smiled. He tipped his hat, regarded her auburn hair.

"Howdy."

"Welcome to Belleville and the Palace."

"Thanks, ma'am."

"I'm Laurie. Laurie Whiston. I'll have a drink

with you, if you're buying."

"I'm buying."

"Whiskey?"

"If you like. Barkeep, a whiskey for the lady. Leave the bottle."

"My, you know how to treat a lady."

Buck pulled out his poke as the bartender brought the bottle, an extra glass.

"I've only got dust. No coin."

"Dan can change it for you," she said. She gestured to the bartender. He brought scales, measuring weights.

"How much you want to change?" asked Dan, a slab-chested Irishman with a balding head, thick, brushy moustache.

Buck poured out a pile of grains.

"What're you paying?"

"Sixteen dollars to the ounce. Same as in San Bernardino."

Dan put weights on the scale to match the small pile of dust. Wordlessly, he counted out sixty-five dollars.

"A shade over four ounces," he said.

"Fair enough," said Buck, leaving five dollars on the bar, pocketing his poke and the bills.

Buck lifted his glass in a toast. He knew that she would not drink the whiskey she had ordered, but she might provide him some information. She put the glass to her lips, but did not swallow any. He knew how she had to make a living and did not fault her for that.

"You're not a miner," Laurie said.

"No'm."

70

"Not much to do up here unless you prospect or work for wages."

He looked at her a long moment.

She set her glass on the bar. Buck slid his over beside it, half empty.

"Some would argue you that, Miss."

"Laurie. Call me Laurie."

He nodded. He continued to scan the room. He was satisfied that some of the curiosity about himself had worn off. The room buzzed with idle conversation, with talk of the hanging, of gold, of Lucky Baldwin and the rush of fifty-nine. He noticed the big man at the far corner who was sitting with other men, but somehow dominating them with his presence. More than once, Buck had felt the big man's eyes on him. The man looked as if he belonged there, as if he was holding court. He looked, in fact, as if he either owned the place or was a permanent fixture there.

"That's Mister Singleton," said Laurie, as if reading Buck's thoughts. "Bert Singleton. He owns the Palace."

"He been away lately?"

"No," she said, slightly puzzled, "why?"

"I'm looking for someone I saw recently."

"Maybe I can help. I know most everybody who comes in here."

Buck looked at her. She just might know most everybody who passed through Belleville.

"Did you happen to see four men ride in last night, or this morning?"

"No," she said, after pausing to think a few

seconds. "Not four men all in a bunch. A lot of people ride back and forth through these mountains. From Union Flat, Starvation Flat, Coyote Flat, San Bernardino, Colton, Los Angeles, Victor, Barstow.

"One man dressed like a Californio, but he was no Spaniard nor Mexican. Another was a young lad, light-haired, rangy. One of them sounded like a cash box when he walked."

"And the fourth man?"

"I don't know about him," he said. "Didn't get a good look. He was tall, big. Could have been anybody."

"The one you said sounded like a cash box when he walked. That could be Jingles."

"Jingles?"

Laurie laughed, her voice deep and throaty.

"Shh! Not so loud." Her voice dropped to a confidential tone. "That's what they call him. He's seldom in town, but most everyone here has some kind of nickname. This man carries a lot of loose silver in his pockets. He sounds like what you said when he walks. Jingles. He makes a lot of noise, when he comes in here, both with his mouth and with his money."

"He has money, then?"

"Yes. He's always playing with silver dollars, but he spends greenbacks."

"Does he have a last name?"

"Reep, I think. I don't know his given name. Jingles . . . Reep."

"Thanks," said Buck. "Know where I might find him about now?"

72

She thought about it for a moment.

"No, and speaking of names, I didn't catch yours."

"Sorry. It's Buck. Jess Buck."

"And you're from Texas?"

He grinned.

"A long time ago. Does it show?"

"It sounds. Your talk. Yeah, I guess it shows too. They call you Jess?"

"Buck or Jess. I answer to either one."

Laurie gave him a new look of appraisal. He didn't look like most of the men she'd seen who were on the run. He was trail-weathered, but not untidy. He could use a bath and a razor. He looked sure of himself, and his right hand never stayed long on the bar, but kept floating off to his side, near the butt of his pistol.

Buck felt her eyes on him, let her look him over. He was busy with thoughts of his own.

He had no doubt that Laurie Whiston had been sent to talk to him, find out who he was. No matter. He liked her. She was pretty and she was helpful. She had given him a name. He might be able to do something with that name. One name could lead to another name. And, that name to still another.

"This Reep feller. Would he be staying in town?"

"No, I don't think so. He stays out in the hills most of the time. He's got the reputation of being just a shade outside the law."

Buck made no comment, but finished off his whiskey.

"Anything else you want to know?" she asked.

"Yes," he said, "one thing. Without pointing, could you tell me in which direction I'm likely to find Reep?"

She told him.

Now he had a name and a place.

It was more than he had when he had come into town.

"Much obliged," he said. "I'll be going now."

He tipped his hat, started toward the hotel lobby.

Before he reached the doorway, a man stepped away from the bar, grabbed his arm.

Buck turned, went into a crouch.

His hand flew to the butt of his pistol.

CHAPTER SEVEN

Julio Machado released his grip on Buck's arm.

Laurie Whiston's mouth dropped open. A low murmur filled the room as men saw the stranger go for his gun.

Machado smiled, showed his empty hands.

"You are too fast, *Senor,*" he said, "but please do not draw your pistol. I mean you no harm."

"Man oughtn't to come up like that, grab my arm."

"Pardon, amigo."

Buck stood up straight, relaxed. His gun hand floated above his holster. The crowd settled down, the murmur died away. But men had noticed the stranger's quickness.

"State your business," said Buck.

"I am Julio Machado. I work for Lucky Foster. He is one of the biggest mine owners in these parts."

"I don't know the man."

"He asked me to see you, invite you to his ranch. He wishes to talk to you."

"I thought you said he owned a mine."

"And a ranch," said Machado cordially.

"What's he want?"

"I do not know. He saw you at the hanging this afternoon."

Machado looked at Buck's pistol.

"I'm busy."

"I'm sure you will not regret the ride. But I would like to tell him your name and that you will come."

Buck thought it over. He knew no one here. Laurie Whiston was the only person he had spoken to. He had nothing to lose, perhaps something to gain. It sounded as though Foster might be someone to know.

"The name's Jess Buck."

"Ah." Again Machado's gaze fixed on Buck's pistol.

Buck caught his look. There was something about Machado that bothered him. He couldn't pin it down. Julio was friendly enough, but there seemed to be something back of his words. Something that he ought to know about.

"When?" asked Buck.

"As soon as possible."

"How do I get out there?"

Machado told him.

"I'll be there as soon as I get some duds, scrape my face."

Machado touched the brim of his hat.

"I will tell Mister Foster you are coming. *Adios*. We will meet again."

Without another word, Machado walked across the room and through the lobby of the hotel. Something vaguely familiar about him made Buck watch him extra closely. He was certain he had never seen the man before, but there was something in his bearing that reminded Buck of someone or someplace.

He shook off the feeling.

Thoughts of Reep returned. His own business had to come first. Reep and his friends had taken his horse, rifle, pistol, and saddlebags. In those bags was almost $8000 of his money. Money that he'd worked three years for and needed badly. He'd done a lot of riding and a lot of trading to earn that money. He wasn't about to see it disappear into the pockets of outlaws.

He glanced over to look once more at Laurie, say a final farewell.

But she was gone.

He turned and saw her walking toward the table in back, the one where the man named Singleton held court. Another man was heading in the same direction. Tied down pistol rig, tight clothes. Buck tagged him with a single glance.

Gunfighter.

He shrugged, walked toward the lobby, the whiskey in his belly warming him, whetting his appetite.

Vern Slatter reached Singleton's table before Laurie.

"What do you make of him?" asked Singleton.

Slatter scowled.

"Quick. Not nervous. Just quick."

"You better explain that."

"He has eyes all over his head."

"Dammit, Slatter, tell it straight."

"I wouldn't come up too close to him from the front."

Bert Singleton made a sound as he hissed air through his teeth. He understood. Vern was a professional. He knew his business.

Laurie Whiston eased into a chair, looked at her boss.

"Well, Laurie?" asked Singleton.

"He's looking for someone. Reep and his cronies."

"Reep?"

"I think so. I don't know why. He—he's not easy to talk to." A wistful look passed over her face, clouded her eyes.

Singleton's brow knitted in thought.

He didn't like to make mistakes. Bert was a slow thinker, but a sure one. He had come up the hard way and was still going up fast enough to want to reach the top. He drove himself because the memories of Starvation Flat and five dollars a day in dust after backbreaking work still lingered in his mind. He had finally realized that the money earned from a pan never stuck to the fingers of the man who panned it, but to the enterprising man who knew how to entertain and extract that gold from the prospector's leather pouch. He had survived because he was strong and tough and smart. And, because he knew men and the way they thought. Most men. He made it a point to judge each one he met. Some of these men he could use, some he could dominate.

Singleton wanted to know what kind of man Jess Buck was. He also wanted to know why he had come to Belleville. The shadows were already long across the Holcomb Valley, filling the crevices of the ramshackle buildings with portent. There was not much more to be gotten here. The Mother Lode had never been found and though talk ran high, no one was likely to find it. That big vein of gold was as elusive as quicksilver.

His face turned ruddy as he cleared his throat. His veins bulged in his neck. He gripped a lit cigar in his hands, brought it to his mouth. He drew the smoke into his mouth, swirled it around and spewed it into the air above his head as he tilted backwards.

"What do you think, Vern?" he asked, never looking at Slatter.

"Appears to me he's some kind of hardcase."

"He on the run?"

"Don't look that way to me. Mebbe been on the owlhoot a time or so, but not now. He's runnin', but not from the law. Mebbe after somethin'. Or someone."

Bert's gaze focused on Laurie.

Her eyebrows arched and her shoulders shrugged slightly.

"That's the way he looks to me, too," she said. "And he asked about Jingles. He looks as if he's in pain. I saw him . . . well, he looked kind of hurt."

"What do you mean?" asked Singleton.

"Oh, I don't really know. Something in his

79

eyes. Something about the way he stood and moved. Like he had been hurt, or had something broken."

"You looked at him pretty close," said her boss, an edge to his voice.

"Bert . . . ."

Singleton's mouth became a bellows to his cigar again. Smoke wreathed the air over the table. He looked at Vern.

"Think he could be useful to us?"

"Hard tellin'," said Slatter, warily. His eyes never focused on anything for long. He had been down the pike and a man like Vern made enemies. He knew that. He was always looking for something out of place.

"He might be a good man," ventured Singleton.

No one said anything.

Bert stubbed out his cigar in Slatter's whiskey. The liquid hissed.

"We gotta talk to someone else about him first," said Singleton. "But he might do. He just might do."

"Yeah," said Vern, nervously. "I know what you mean."

"Laurie, you better get back to work before people talk," said her employer. "You keep your eyes peeled right sharp."

He didn't look at her, see her cringe with self-loathing.

Slatter ignored her, too, his eyes fixed for a moment on Singleton's fleshy face. Singleton waved Laurie Whiston away and she rose from the table with a dazed look on her face, her shoulders sagging.

A moment later, she began circulating through the room, slapping men on their backs, saying hello, laughing at a joke, curtseying at a compliment.

Singleton watched her for a moment, then turned his attention to Slatter.

The two men began conversing in low tones.

Laurie paused, looked back at the table.

She shuddered, knowing that a man named Jess Buck was caught in a web, even though he didn't know it.

The deck had been opened, shuffled, and soon, someone would be dealing cards out to all the players.

The Foster Ranch lay in a far corner of the valley, rich with grass, framed by pines and spruce. Stock cattle grazed, a horse nickered as he rode up through the meadow to the main house. It was the first place he'd seen up in the mountains that wasn't laced with placer diggings. Belleville itself was surrounded by mounds and ponds, channels dug from creeks. Even in the center of town, men worked the earth for its gold, the arrastres grinding the raw ore with mule power.

Buck rode up to the hitchrail, dismounted. He had seen no one and now, only the breeze stirred up sound in the afternoon. The log home was huge, tidy, impressive. He saw a corral off through the trees, buildings visible on the slope above the meadow surrounding the house. Ground squirrels scurried over the rocks that bordered the field. A grey squirrel chittered noisily in a pine by the side of the house.

He walked up the steps, across the wide porch, his boots making hollow sounds in the wood. He knocked on the door, waited.

He heard movement, the door opened.

Buck sucked in a breath.

The girl was beautiful, young. She wore a blue gingham dress with white piping. She had dark hair and deep brown eyes, rosy natural cheeks and a full bosom. He took her to be about twenty, a year less or a year more. She smiled at him with even teeth and dimples burrowed into the corners of her mouth. He took off his hat.

"Afternoon, ma'am. I'm Jess Buck. Mister Foster asked me to stop by."

"Yes. Come in, Mister Buck. I'm Amy Foster, his daughter. He's in the study. I'll tell him you're here."

He waited in a hallway outside a large living room furnished with hardwood Spanish-style furniture. In a moment, Amy reappeared.

"He'll see you now. Just follow me."

The study was off the main room, lined with bookshelves, hunting trophies, rifles and pistols on the walls. It was a man's room. Foster sat in a dyed cowhide chair that was big but didn't swallow him up.

"Glad you could make it out," said Foster, standing up, stretching out his hand. "You've met my daughter, Amy."

Buck nodded, shook Foster's hand.

"Jess Buck, eh? Well, sit down, make yourself to home."

Foster waved Buck to a chair that was not quite as large as the one he was in, but big enough, comfortable.

Buck was glad that he had taken the time to buy new duds, scrape his face. He felt Amy's eyes scanning him. She stood there for a moment, smiled, then left the two men to talk.

The two men looked at each other appraisingly.

Foster was taller than Buck, with greying hair at his temples, no fat on his frame and eyes like Amy's. But harder and darker. His clothes were well-cut and neat, but his hands showed hard-work callouses. He had a high forehead, few wrinkles. His face was tanned, and he had dimples near the corners of his mouth, like Amy's, only his seemed to have been chipped out of granite and were there whether he smiled or not.

"Well, Buck, I've got a proposition for you, if you're going to be around Belleville for a spell. Have a drink?"

Buck nodded. Foster rose and brought a bottle of good whiskey and a thick crystal glass. Buck held the glass and Foster poured a generous draught into it.

"I'm a stranger here," said Buck, who noticed that Foster didn't take a drink for himself. "You don't know anything about me."

83

Foster sat back down and moved his lips so that the top one folded underneath the bottom one.

"You're right. I don't know much about you. But I know men and my man, Machado agrees with me. You met him."

"Yes."

"Machado doesn't make many mistakes. He—he's a sort of foreman for me, but not in ranching or mining. I call him a—a kind of trouble-shooter."

"He's a gun."

"If you want to put it that way. Bodyguard. Segundo. He, ah, sees to it that things run smoothly in my operations."

Buck said nothing. He held his glass, without drinking from it. He wanted to size up Foster and wanted no distractions.

"Machado thought you might be willing to work for me on somewhat the same basis. He can't handle it by his lonesome."

Buck leaned back in the chair, took a swallow of the whiskey. It was good whiskey, smooth with no tobacco or dog hair in it.

"I doubt I'm your man, Mister Foster."

Foster's eyebrows went up, but came quickly down. His dimples deepened, hardened.

"It might tide you over until you find something better. Until you find who you're looking for."

It was Buck's turn to be surprised.

"Who said I was looking for anybody?"

"I saw you at the hanging. You looked those boys over pretty good. No accounts. Dumb."

"What'd they do?"

"Claim jumpers. Stupid bastards."

Buck finished his drink. His eyes watered. The second drink made him realize the potency of the whiskey. Smooth, but full of fire.

"What's your deal, Mister Foster? Exactly?" Buck's eyes narrowed and he set his glass down on a sidetable.

Foster looked at Buck shrewdly, as if framing his words before he replied.

"Exactly this. There's something stewing here in Holcomb Valley. It's boom time now, but it's petering out. Every day, less gold. Baldwin's already pulled out and I don't hear the stamp mills working so hard. There's land here, though, and a good future for men who see beyond the diggings. Some men are trying to grab all they can. Money, gold, land, whatever. Oh, some men are set, like Van Duzen, Holcomb, some others. But other men, I won't say who, just yet, are after all of it. Those four men might have been part of it. Hired by some who don't want their faces seen. That's my hunch. I think it's going to get worse up here. It might get down to something other than pieces of paper and money changing hands. Follow me?"

"Maybe. I've seen such things happen before. Men come into a place and it looks good for a while. Then, the squabbles start. Water, land, gold. It doesn't make much difference. If one man has, another wants."

"Right." Foster smiled warmly at Buck. "Now, I've got a few men here, not many, and none of them can handle themselves like Julio Machado. But he's just one man. I need someone to back him up in case there's trouble."

"Would you, Mister Foster," Buck asked slowly, "be one of those men who wants to grab up everything?"

His words hung in the air like smoke. Foster's eyes closed to slits.

"Not in the way you mean, Buck," Foster said evenly. "I mean to stay here and I mean to protect my holdings. I have the feeling, though, that I'm being caught in a squeeze by certain men of the kind I've mentioned."

"How so?"

"Oh, it's just a gut feeling at this point. There's a change in the wind. New faces around the town and up here in the valley. Land claims changing hands faster'n we can keep track of them. In San Bernardino, down the hill, the land office has a lot of new names holding title to land we were planning to acquire. It's not simple and I can't go into all the details right now. All of this is very recent, but I expect things'll come to a head pretty soon."

"So, you want me as a gunny alongside your Machado."

It was a flat statement. Buck stared at Foster. The rancher did not swerve his glance.

"Well," he said, "you are a *pistolero,* aren't you?"

Buck's back stiffened when he heard the word.

That was the second time in a week he'd heard that term. It didn't belong here, somehow. It

86

belonged back in Texas, back when he was young. He felt the hairs on the back of his neck rise.

His mind began grasping for something that was just out of reach. For something he had to know, had to remember.

CHAPTER EIGHT

Even before Buck opened his mouth, Foster knew his answer.

"I'm no *pistolero*, Mister Foster," said Buck. "I left those days behind in Texas. But I guess you can't be much different from what folks want you to be."

Foster didn't flinch.

"You came here looking for someone. I don't figure it's me or you wouldn't have walked in here. But I won't argue with you. Maybe I made a mistake, calling you a *pistolero*, but you'll use the pistol and I just want to make sure it's on the right side. If you use it. With me, you may not have to."

"But I might. And I don't mind using it if I have to, but I don't want to hire out my gun."

"I'm sorry you feel that way. I thought we might work together."

"Thanks for you offer. I've got a thing to do and I don't want any hobbles."

"If you change your mind . . . you're the kind of man I'm looking for. I've got enough of the other kind. I need someone who can stand up to. . . ." His words trailed off.

Lucky did everything he could to keep from biting his lip. He had almost said too much. Perhaps he had. At any rate, he would have to keep an eye on Buck. There were others, he was sure who would pay as much or more for that gun than he was prepared to offer. The information he had on Buck was good enough, he was sure, to make that estimate of him. He could use that Colt on his gunbelt. He had noticed, too, that Buck did everything with his left hand, yet his pistol rode on his right hip. He was a gunslinger, all right, or Lucky missed his guess.

The two men shook hands and Buck strode out of the room. Amy rose from her chair in the livingroom.

"Are we going to see more of you, Mister Buck?"

"I turned down your father's offer, if that's what you mean?"

She looked taken aback.

"Are you sure you won't reconsider?"

"No ma'am. I'm not looking for a job."

"I see."

"I'll be leaving ma'am," he said, shifting his weight.

"Yes. I'll show you out."

He followed her to the door, puzzled. Somehow, she had seemed relieved when he had told her he had turned down her father's offer. He wondered why. At the door, she opened it, looked up at him.

"Was it Machado?" she asked, her voice low, confidential.

"No. I don't know him."

"I don't like him," she said quickly, looking around to see if anyone had overheard. "Pa sets store by him, but I think he's . . ." Her voice trailed off.

"Yes?"

"No, I shouldn't have said what I did. Goodbye, Mister Buck. I hope you'll stop by again. You have a standing invitation—from me."

Buck put on his hat.

"Thank you, Miss Foster. I can't say if I'll be back or not. We may meet again. I hope so."

And then he was gone, up on his horse, riding off through the shadow-latticed meadow. The sun was sinking fast over the rim of the high peaks. Night came early in the high country. A breeze rose up, suddenly chill as the sun sank even more. The night bats came out, started to skate in wide circles before he reached Belleville. The squirrels and quail went suddenly silent and the sound of his horse's hooves sounded oddly loud in the silence.

He was disappointed in Foster's offer, but he didn't fault the man for trying. Foster was looking for a gunslinger and Buck had to admit that he fit the description. But he had never hired out his gun, nor would he, ever. He had promised himself that. He had used his gun, yes. Many times. But he had used it only when someone had come gunning for him or used a gun to intimidate others less powerful than he. He had, in recent years, tried to avoid gunplay. It was seldom possible when men who lived by the gun crossed his path. Like that time in Fort Stockton.

A kid had come into the bar full of whiskey and hate. He'd called Buck out and Buck told him to sleep it off. Then the kid had told Buck he'd come to take away his reputation.

"I don't have any reputation," Buck had said.

"You're Jess Buck, ain't you?"

"That I am. And a peaceable man to boot."

"The Jess Buck I heard about has got some marks on his guns."

"Necessary, boy."

"I aim to take 'em away from you."

The kid's eyes were crazy red. His hand hovered over his pistol and he kept goading Jess to draw. Buck kept talking, trying to calm the youth down, and never moved his hand. Not once.

Then the kid, when the men at the bar began laughing at him, couldn't stand it any more. That's when his hand moved to his gun. That's when Buck had gone into his crouch, faster than anyone could track. In no more time than it takes a wing to beat, his hand had sped to the butt of his pistol. It was out of the leather before the kid could cock his hammer.

Jess shot so fast he didn't have time to aim for a wounding shot. The kid dropped like a stone with a bullet through his gullet.

And Buck had to move on, with another uncut notch on his pistol, another killing to follow him across the wide country.

Things like that made him wish he'd never killed that first man.

Yet, more than once, he would have been killed himself if he hadn't been the one to kill first. It was enough to make a man careful of how he acted and who he gave his name out to. Some people had that funny kind of memory that scavenged over some things like vultures worrying carrion.

He had hoped it would be different in this country.

But now, four men had robbed him, left him to die. They had to be called out to answer for it. They had left him without water or a horse. It was not a good thing to let go by. The reputation would remain and he was still out eight thousand dollars.

And, someone here would have heard of him, remembered who he was. Maybe Machado was one who did.

If Reep and the others were up here, as he believed them to be, then he'd have to use his gun again. It would make the world a whole lot smaller than it was, all right. And pretty soon, somebody would come up on him when he wasn't ready and. . . .

He didn't want to think of that.

Buck picked his way around the darkening sluice boxes and mining equipment as he rode into Belleville. It was dark by the time he rode through the main part of town. Orange lights from oil lamps flickered from buildings in the town, from houses scattered around the hillsides.

The town looked lonesome and homey at the same time and he thought of Amy Foster back at the ranch. She'd be a woman for a man. Not him. He'd had that dream once. To find a place, settle in and get to marrying a good woman, raising kids. He wondered if he'd ever have that old dream. It didn't seem possible now. It had seemed possible when he rode out of Prescott, heading for new country where no one knew him, where he could take his stake and start out fresh.

He rode to the livery stable and put up the blue roan for a reasonable fee. Kevin Whitaker, the stable boy, took his horse and led the animal to the watering trough. Belleville wasn't as outrageous as some towns about prices, but it was high enough for a man with little money. Buck figured he could last a week, week and a half, with the gold he had left—if he watched himself. Then, he'd have to ride to the Pueblo and see if his credit was any good, or hire out for forty a month and found. He shuddered at the thought. He'd worked hard and kept his nose to the grindstone for three years. It was hard for a man to go back when he looked straight ahead.

The Palace was booming with trade when Buck walked up to the porch. It was more full than it had been that afternoon. There was an excitement in the air like a Saturday night and Buck had to remind himself that it was only Wednesday. He walked up to the desk before going into the saloon.

"Yes sir?" The clerk was a different one than when Buck had checked in.

"A couple of cigars. Two of those cheroots."

"Two bits."

Buck winced, but paid up.

He bit the end off one, stuck the other in his shirt pocket. He walked into the bar. He was hungry now and he'd a mind to have a drink and a good meal before turning in.

Music floated above the din of voices and tinkling glasses. A tinny piano at the far end tried gamely to rise above the chatter, accompanied by a tambor and someone scratching a fiddle. It wasn't much, that music, but it added to the excitement somehow. One grizzled old man played a squeezebox, another blew into a harmonica. Buck saw them, but he heard only the drum, piano and fiddle. He saw a guitar player sitting on a stool, tuning up. The music, now that he heard it more clearly, had a lot of sadness in it.

Several glitter gals in bright, brief garments, fishnet stockings or silk, flitted around the room, though some were already settled next to men carrying large enough pokes to assure the girls' undying attentions for the remainder of the evening.

Every table was crammed with customers, and the long bar was stacked with men washing the dust down their throats. The riffle of cards and the clink of chips and coins added to the din. Singleton was there, talking to a group of men at the bar, as was Vern Slatter, who leaned against a back doorway watching the action. Laurie, as hostess for the Palace, flitted through the throng, stopping at each table, seeing that everyone was happy, that the drinks kept flowing.

Buck made his way to an empty spot at the bar, trying his best not to be noticed.

But Slatter noticed him.

So did Singleton, when he looked up.

Laurie, too, saw him, because she tried to see everyone who came into the saloon.

So did another man, whose jaw went slack as he watched the tall man stride to the bar.

The man had stopped in for a quick drink and hadn't meant to stay as long as he had, for he had business elsewhere. His blood turned icy when he saw Buck and he turned his face quickly away. He huddled in between two men on either side of him at the bar, swallowed the last ounce of whiskey in his glass.

He waited until Buck ordered, then turned to leave, hoping he would not be seen.

Buck glanced up at the mirror behind the bar, saw movement.

Then he saw the man's face.

He knew the face.

Buck turned from the bar and stepped out a pace, staring at the man walking toward him.

The man looked up, then, saw Buck standing there. He froze in his tracks, locked his gaze on Buck's.

Some of the others at the bar and nearby tables noticed the two men isolated from the rest, standing twenty paces from each other.

A murmur rose, traveled through the room.

The music stopped.

Cards fell flat on felt tabletops. Chips slid

from fingers.

Men rubbernecked to see, without moving from their places.

"It's Mert Pentell," someone whispered aloud.

"And a stranger," said another.

Buck heard the voices.

Now he knew the name of the man he faced.

CHAPTER NINE

Mert Pentell.

One of the four men who had robbed Jess Buck, left him without food or water or arms. Left him to die.

Buck took a deep breath and stood with his weight balanced evenly on both feet.

His right hand hovered four inches over the butt of his pistol. His eyes narrowed. His jaw hardened until a muscle rippled under the skin.

Singleton, his face flushed until it looked like raw meat, watched the two men square off.

So did everyone else who could see without moving.

The tension crackled like silent lightning.

Mouths went dry as the people realized that one man, perhaps two, was close to death. Pentell's gunhand, too, froze above his pistol butt like a motionless claw.

"I don't want no trouble here, mister," said Pentell.

"You got trouble, Pentell," Buck rasped.

"I don't know you, stranger."

"That some of my money you're spending here?"

"I — I don't know what you're talking about."

"You're a goddamned liar."

Pentell's face drained of color as if swatted with a wet cowhide.

"Mister, I never laid eyes on you before."

"You stole from me and set me afoot in the desert. That's bad medicine where I come from, Pentell."

Pentell's mouth went dry. His face turned ashen.

But he didn't deny Buck's charges.

A low whisper started at one table, rose to a murmur as the silence grew between the two men.

Pentell licked his lips.

Buck watched his eyes. Only his eyes.

They flickered ever so slightly.

Buck went into a half-crouch, his hand stabbing downward. Pentell's hand had already started moving toward his pistol.

Buck's fingers closed around his pistol butt. The Colt seemed to emerge from his holster of its own volition. The draw was smooth, effortless. A gasp rose up among the nearby spectators. Men standing close at the bar opened their eyes wide, staring in disbelief.

Pentell's face darkened. The veins in his neck bulged in relief. He tried to clear leather even as he heard Buck's hammer cocking.

Buck's pistol roared, quivered in his hand.

Smoke and flame belched from the barrel.

Someone yelled a warning to Pentell.

But the gunman knew he was too late.

Even as his finger squeezed the trigger a split second before his pistol was level.

The bullet from Buck's gun rammed into Pentell's gut just above his belt buckle. His body twitched. A crimson stain spread across his middle. The ball ripped through his back, gouging out a fist-sized hole as his own pistol boomed. The shot from Pentell's gun tore splinters from the floor just in front of Buck's boots.

Pentell's eyes glazed over with the mist of impending death.

His body sagged. Muscles rippled involuntarily.

Buck cocked his pistol again, ready to fire again if it became necessary.

Pentell tried to hold his footing, but his knees buckled. Air rushed out of his mouth.

"Christ," someone said.

The outlaw looked around him, wild-eyed, then his fingers opened. His pistol clattered on the floor as it struck. He pitched sideways, his knees finally giving out on him. He stretched out an arm, grunted as the weight of his torso hit the floor with a muffled thud.

Buck stalked warily to the fallen man and bent down. He lifted Pentell's head in his hand and spoke to him. His pistol barrel kept the space around him swept of encroachers. He looked into the dying man's eyes, saw the glaze brought on by pain and shock.

"Pentell, you haven't got much time. I need

some answers."

Pentell groaned. His lips clamped together tightly.

"Why, man? Why did you rob me and leave me out there to die?"

A trickle of blood seeped out of the corner of the gunshot man's mouth.

Buck drew in a breath.

"Come on, man, talk."

Pentell's mouth opened, but no sound came out.

"Pentell, hurry. Who were the others?"

"L—Lost star . . . sssssss. . . ." he gasped.

Buck leaned closer. He had barely heard Pentell. Men crowded in closer to the two men, straining to hear.

"Who was the fourth man?"

Pentell moaned and the breath hissed out of him. Buck shook his head, let Pentell's trunk sag back to the floor. He stood up, holstering his pistol. He turned to face the crowd.

"He didn't make it," he said simply.

"Well, it was a fair fight," said Greek George, a local character who still lived over on Starvation Flat, worked the stream that came down off the mountain.

A number of men murmured assent with George's comment. Buck nodded, strode to the bar, satisfied.

Some of the men dragged Pentell's body out the back door, while others went to fetch a wagon. There was no undertaker in Belleville. Someone would bury him and probably no one would be interested in where he was buried.

Bert Singleton sidled up to Buck at the bar.

"You had some trouble with Pentell before?" he asked, his face beefy red, clouded in cigar smoke.

"He and three others robbed me the other day and left me without horse nor water nor weapon," said Buck simply.

"Well, I'd like to shake your hand, stranger. I'm Bert Singleton, the owner of this establishment, and the house is yours tonight. Drink all you want and eat the same."

"Thanks, Singleton. Jess Buck's my name and I'm grateful for the hospitality."

Singleton grinned wide.

"I liked the way you handled that business, Buck," he said, through a haze of cigar smoke. He towered over Buck when he stood straight up, but he was leaning on the bar so that the two men's eyes were on a level. The hubbub in the room picked up again as before. "Pentell had some reputation with a gun. They said he was on the fast side."

"Maybe I had more at stake than Pentell."

"You could have lost your temper and gone *loco*. You say he robbed you?"

"A considerable poke. Several thousand in greenbacks and gold."

Singleton let out a whistle. His brows knit as he continued to puff cloudlets of smoke into the air.

"I don't hold with a man being set afoot in the desert without water," said the big man. "I'd say you were lucky to get out alive. Mighty lucky."

One of the local citizens came up, then, and

spoke to Singleton. He was a member of the Vigilante's Committee, Earl Dobbs, the owner of a general store in Belleville.

"Bert, was it a fair fight?" asked Dobbs.

"Yes, Earl. Meet Jess Buck. Earl Dobbs, Buck. Look, Earl, Pentell was a thief. He robbed Buck here. Anyway, Pentell drew first. Buck just came out on top."

"Yeah. All right, Bert. Had to be sure."

Dobbs shot a look in Buck's direction. He didn't offer his hand before he walked away.

"He looks disappointed. Vigilante?"

"Yes," said Singleton quickly, as if embarrassed. "Law's scarce up here. Constable Holcomb comes up once in a while.

Buck said nothing. He recognized Dobbs as the man who had fired the pistol that afternoon, sending four men to their deaths at the end of four ropes. It was likely Dobbs enjoyed such doings and Buck was glad the man hadn't offered his hand. He would have refused to shake it.

"We try to keep a lawful town, Buck," Singleton explained after Dobbs was out of earshot. "But, tell me, was Pentell the only one of the robbers you knew?"

"I didn't know him, never saw him but twice. Once when he robbed me and a few minutes ago. There were four men."

"Then that means you'll be looking for the other three. You track them here?"

"I did. I know the name of one of the others. I'll recognize another. But the fourth man. . . ."

"You didn't see him?"

"I saw him, but he was too far away to make out his features. I take him for the ramrod." Buck sipped the last of his drink and waved away the bartender who began to pour another.

"Hmm," said Singleton, worrying his cigar in sausage fingers, "looks as though you'll be around a spell. Buck, I'd like to make you an offer."

Buck studied Singleton, wondering what had prompted this latest proposition.

"Yes?"

"How'd you like to earn some money while you're looking for those other men?"

"I'm comfortable for a while. A week or so. Figure it won't take that long once I get my bearings."

"I could use a gun like yours."

"That's what I thought," said Buck. "I don't hire out my gun, Singleton."

The saloon owner's face reddened and he coughed phlegmatically. He wasn't prepared for Buck's quick negative answer.

"You use that Colt well enough, I'm thinking."

"I just don't hire out."

Singleton cleared his throat loudly, tossed down his drink. He glanced at the back door where Slatter lounged against the wall. Then, he turned his back to Buck, his eyes narrowed to puffy slits.

"It might help if you did, Buck. It would kind of put you on the right side, if you know what I mean."

"Look, Singleton, I feel bad about running

103

into Pentell in your saloon. I didn't look for gunplay nor did I expect Pentell or any of the others would be here tonight. I don't know what kind of law you got here, but I've seen vigilantes get worse than rattlesnakes when they go on the prod. They say they're upholding the law, but you got to ask whose law and if it's their law well they're mostly hemp-happy and trigger-quick.

"I don't aim to get myself a rope from your welcoming committee, but the men who robbed me came here. They've got my money and I want it back."

"You talk real hardheaded, Buck."

"May be, Singleton. But the answer's final. I don't hire out my gun and I don't move much when I'm pushed."

The words hung between the two men. Buck didn't take his eyes off Singleton's.

It was Singleton who broke the gaze first. He garrumphed and turned away from Buck.

"I hope you find what you're looking for quick," he said over his shoulder.

Buck watched him walk toward the back. Toward the man leaning against the wall. He turned to the bartender, motioned him over.

"What's the name of that man back there talking to Singleton?"

"Vern Slatter. You don't want to . . . well, none of my business, but Slatter's pure poison."

"Thanks. I'll keep that in mind."

Buck knew what kind of man Slatter was. He'd seen them in every dirtwater, shanty town from the Texas border to the Pacific Ocean.

Gunfighter.

He wondered if he would have to take his gun out against Slatter.

It seemed certain just then that he would as he walked out of the saloon.

Much as he regretted it, he knew he had an enemy in Bert Singleton.

CHAPTER TEN

Lost Star.

Buck couldn't get the words out of his mind. They had to mean something. Pentell had been a dying man when he'd said them, and he knew he was dying. A man didn't often waste his last words.

But he hadn't said the name of that fourth man.

Or had he? Maybe the man he was looking for had something to do with a star. But what was a lost star? It didn't make sense. But it had made sense to Pentell. It must have been mighty important to him.

Maybe, though, Pentell had feared his leader so much he couldn't bring himself to say his name. Yet, there had been some of what he'd had to say that Buck had missed. A sound, part of a name or a word. Something. Maybe.

He kicked off his boots and lay back on the bed in his room. He was stuffed with steak and potatoes, milk and strong coffee. But he hadn't eaten at the Palace. He had found a cafe at the edge of town that was open, filled with the talk of bragging miners, talk of the hanging and no mention of the shooting at Singleton's. He felt damned good, despite the fact that he'd had to kill another man.

He was dog tired, but sparked up with an excitement he couldn't explain. He felt he was getting closer to the men he sought. Closer than he had been a day ago.

When the knock came, he jumped, as if almost expecting it.

He slid his pistol out of his holster, stood up in stocking feet.

The Colt was cleaned, reloaded.

He walked to the door, stood to one side as he called out.

"Who's there?"

"It's me, Laurie." Voice just above a whisper. A tone of urgency in it.

He opened the door.

Laurie slipped quickly inside his room, her skirts rustling across the bare floor. Buck holstered his pistol and looked at her in puzzlement. He didn't figure Laurie for being this bold, coming to a lone man's room uninvited. But he held back final judgment of her actions until he had heard her out. Either way, she was taking some chance.

In the light of the oil lamps, Laurie's hair shone like copper. Buck gave her a closer appraisal than he'd given her before and relaxed his wide shoulders as he gestured to the only chair in the room.

She looked at his lean, strong-boned face and flashed a tentative smile.

"Thanks," she said, "but I can't stay but a minute. I — I thought you might like to know something."

Buck leaned against the wall near the door, his eyes bright, interested.

"Sure, Laurie. I appreciate it."

"There's talk downstairs. Ugly talk. After you — you shot that man, well, Dobbs came back and brought some other men with him. Some of the vigilantes."

Buck's eyebrows arched.

"These men have names? You know them?"

"Randy Falconer's one. Percy Jensen. Jensen is a lot like Dobbs. He likes nothing better than a hanging. Falconer tries to be fair-minded, but he's usually overruled by Dobbs and Jensen."

"That it? Those the vigilantes?" He had met Dobbs and his kind didn't worry him much. By himself, he was not dangerous. In a mob, he would be somewhere in the middle of the pack, where he thought it was safe. But, he was a loudmouth and liked to swing his weight around, if he thought the pack was behind him. That kind didn't bother him. It was the man who believed he was right even when he was wrong that was dangerous, especially if he could persuade others, fence sitters, weaker men, to think his own way. Dobbs didn't fit into that category, he was sure.

"No, Jess Buck, there's Con Houston — a better man than any I've named. He's fair and he doesn't go around with his pistol half-cocked like some of the others. But Con wasn't with the others tonight."

"Just what was in Dobbs' craw?"

"They were talking about how it wasn't safe to let gunfighters hang around town, or to even let them into town in the first place. They said it was best to—to hang them as they rode in." She shivered, went on. "It—it was whiskey talk, but a lot of people started agreeing with them."

Buck's mind raced. A mob. That was where Dobbs thrived. And, it looked like he was trying to stir up a mob. Maybe he wasn't as stupid as he appeared to be.

He looked at Laurie with new respect.

"I surely thank you for telling me this," he said. "I'll try to step real careful."

Laurie started to say something else, but apparently thought better of it. She looked at Buck and smiled wanly, as if trying to make him feel at ease despite her dire message.

"I'll be going now," she said, taking a step toward the door.

"Just a minute, Laurie, if you don't mind," he said, stepping away from the wall.

Her eyes flickered with doubt.

"One question," he said. "Lost Star. Know what it means?"

Laurie cocked her head quizzically. Her eyes seemed to go cloudy.

"I—I don't know," she replied.

"Pentell said it plain—just before he died. It might be important."

"Hmm, it could be . . . there's a lot of talk about such things here."

"What's that?"

"Mines. Gold mines. I've heard the name Lost Star before. At least I think I have. It sounds familiar." She paused, then her eyes flickered as the light caught her head movement. "Van Duzen. Ever hear of him?"

Buck shook his head.

"Not the mana. Road named after him."

"Yes. He found something up here. He and another man, his partner. I don't know any of the details, but there was talk of a lost mine. I think it was called the Lost Star Mine."

Buck felt his heart jump in his chest.

His mouth opened.

Laurie spoke before he could say anything.

"A lot of people would like to know where it is," she said.

"Pentell said it. Maybe he knew."

"That's odd, isn't it? That he'd start to tell you something about that. Why?"

"I don't know, Laurie. But I aim to find out."

Laurie hesitated as if searching her mind for more information. Suddenly, she snapped her fingers.

"There might be somebody who can help you, Jess."

He walked over to her, started to reach out with his hands to grasp her shoulders, thought better of it.

"I'd sure be grateful," he said, shifting his weight onto one foot.

"Moses Purdy. He's an old-timer who lives all by himself, up on Holcomb Creek. He was here from the start, in fifty-nine. Came in with Billy Holcomb and Ben Chateau, the Indian. He knew Van Duzen well. At least he knows the whole story about that lost mine. Maybe he can help you."

"Can you tell me how to get there? Roughly?"

"There's a stream on the west side of the valley, beyond the rocky ridge that rings Belleville. It's called Holcomb Creek. Follow the creek north and you'll find Purdy's cabin. He's built himself a little log shack and he comes into town to weigh out his gold every so often. Some of us girls rode up there last Sunday. You'll find it easy."

"I'm much obliged. Again."

She looked up at him with eyes flickering something more than friendship, just then. He thought she was going to reach out and touch him, but she held fast. Her mouth opened slightly.

"I—I wasn't afraid to come here," she stammered. "I thought about being alone with you, how it would look. I wish I had reason to fear you, but I don't. You—you seem to be a good man, unjustly judged. I wish you well."

He took her hand, then, squeezed it.

"No—I—I really must be going."

She jerked her hand out of his, walked to the door. Then, she stopped, turned to him. Buck was already reaching for the cheroot in his shirt pocket. He put it between his lips, waited for her to speak.

"There's something else I heard, Jess. I almost forgot."

He didn't say anything.

"I overheard Bert . . . Mister Singleton . . . and Vern Slatter. You know them?"

"I've met Singleton."

"Vern works for Mister Singleton. The girls call him a bouncer, but he's really more than that."

"He the one hangs out in the back, lean as a wolf, sniffing trouble?"

"Yes."

"I know which one he is," said Buck quietly.

"It — it may not mean anything, but were you robbed of some money?"

"I was."

A light seemed to spread over Laurie's face.

"You heard something about that?" he asked. So far as he knew he had only told Singleton and Foster.

"Maybe," she said. "Bert — Mister Singleton, told Vern to see to it that you got your money back. I didn't think you'd been playing at any of our tables, so I thought you might have been robbed by that Pentell."

"He was one of four."

"Well, I don't know for sure if they meant *that* money. But Vern left the Palace right after Mister Singleton gave him the order."

Buck let out a breath.

It was puzzling. He didn't recognize Slatter at all. He could have been the fourth man, but somehow he didn't seem the type to command men. The man he sought was powerful. He had the kind of power you could feel at a distance, even without seeing his face. It was in the way he sat his horse, the way he looked at a man over a long distance. Even though you couldn't see the eyes, you could feel them boring into you. Slatter wasn't that kind of man.

Buck pulled his cigar from his mouth. He had bitten it through.

"I'm much obliged again," he said.

"Good night, Jess," she said, opening the door.

"Good night, Laurie. I owe you a favor."

For a fleeting second he thought she was going to come back into the room. She paused there, in the doorway, and a shadow crossed her face, a wistful look came into her eyes. It was there for only an instant and then was gone.

"No," she whispered, "you don't owe me anything."

And then she was gone, her skirts rustling as she walked down the hall. He heard her footsteps fade away on the stairs.

After he closed the door, he drew a deep breath.

Laurie was some kind of woman. She had seen better days, for sure. But for a moment there, he'd felt a yearning that was hard to shake. She was pushing forty, he figured, but that didn't make her less attractive to him. He shook off the feeling. Maybe he had just been grateful or maybe it was because the lamplight in the room wasn't the strongest, the most unflattering, but he had wanted her when she lingered there in the doorway.

He let out a breath, stuck the mashed end of the cheroot back in his mouth.

He shook his head as if to shake off the feeling.

He wondered whether he would have kissed her, if she'd offered.

Maybe.

But Buck knew that if she had come back in the room, he wouldn't have minded at all.

He felt good now, tired enough to sleep.

The sounds on the street died away and he blew out the lamps. He sagged to the bed after shelling out of his clothes. He lay down, knowing his next moves would have to be made quickly.

But Laurie was still on his mind.

He wondered who the town was named after. *Belleville*. Beautiful town, in French. But, maybe named after a pretty girl.

It was a right smart name.

CHAPTER ELEVEN

The sun lit a green world of waving grasses in Holcomb Valley as Buck rode slowly over the gritty road. The crisp mountain air washed against his face and the blue roan stepped out frisky as a spring colt. He had slept well and had arisen before sunup, bear-hungry, rested and refreshed. The bruises had not hurt so much this morning and the cuts and scrapes were healing fast. He jabbed his spurs into the roan's flanks, picking up the pace. The sounds of miners working their claims faded behind him as he rode toward the rocky ridge Laurie had told him about. The road ought to lead him to Holcomb Creek where he would turn and follow it north. The morning dew was beaded up on the grasses, scintillating like diamonds in the sun. At seven thousand feet, the coolness lingered until the sun crept over the valley and burned off the dew with searing fingers of light.

Buck felt better than he had in a week. He'd eaten a breakfast of *bistec ranchero con juevos,* hot *tortillas* made of corn flour, and all of it sprinkled generously with a *salsa picante* that was still peppery in his stomach. There had been few people about at that hour of the morning and he hadn't seen anyone he recognized. It was just as well. After what Laurie had told him it was probably better if he let things simmer down by themselves. Already, events had moved too swiftly to suit him. His mind was crammed with information that needed attention and he'd hardly had time to digest all that he'd heard. The fleeting bits of information floated through his brain but he could not form them into any usable shape or pattern. They were just scraps of confetti that needed to be nailed down, but in order, made sense of.

Maybe Moses Purdy could give him some answers.

The ride to Holcomb Creek was not far. He picked his way past the mining camps on the flats, avoided the voices, the clatter of picks and pans, the bray of the mules, threaded his way through stunted and tall, straight pines, muscular cedars. The creek was low and he saw where beaver had dammed it up to form pools. He saw the flash of a rainbow trout and startled a chipmunk sipping water at its edge. This was fine country, he thought, a good place for a man to settle once the boom had tapered off and the goldseekers scattered to other claims beyond this high valley.

He headed the blue roan upstream after it had nibbled the water at the pool. He crossed it once, twice, then found a narrow road that had been hacked out, traveled, so that it was easy to follow.

116

Trees had been cleared away and stumps dynamited or burned so that a team and wagon could move next to the creek. On the rocks, he saw the high water marks and knew that the creek was down considerably from its spring runoff. Later in the summer, he surmised, the water would go underground and this would appear to be a dry bed. But, there was water running and he saw, somewhat later, that the creek was fed by springs. Water was important and he knew that it could get dry in the mountains just as in the desert. Yet this was a natural place, with considerable water for that time of year. The valley lay in a deep bowl with many streams running into it. The creek flowed well and kept the fish alive that swam up from some lake below.

A man could raise fine cattle in such country, he thought, could put down roots and live right in good clean air.

He saw the cabin, its roof barely visible, through the trees. He clucked to the roan, worked the reins to turn the horse. The shack was made of logs and scrap, clapboard lumber, sat in a clearing that opened up at the mouth of a V created by two ridges. The cabin itself was built of hand-hewn logs, roofed with clapboard lumber, well chinked with burlap, clay and mud. A stove pipe poked up through the roof. There was no smoke.

"Haloooo!" Jess called.

There was no answer and the echoing stillness made him feel certain that the cabin was empty. He dismounted, ground-tied the roan to a stump.

He knocked on the cabin door. The door creaked open and he peered inside. There was no one in the single room. He saw a table, two chairs, a wood sheepherder's stove, kitchen utensils hanging from square nails driven into the wall.

He pulled the door shut, walked off the cluttered porch, took a turn around the cabin. He heard the creek gurgling, a jay scolding a squirrel. He headed down through the wide part of the V between the ridges, back toward the creek.

"Purdy!" he called.

He heard only the burble of the creek from around the bend where the V came together. He walked toward the creek, looking for signs of the man's diggings. Purdy's claim would not be far from the creek, he surmised. The ground was heavily tracked and he followed the packed trail to another ravine that angled off from the creek. There, he found a primitive pole corral, a spring wagon idle next to it. Two mules nibbled at grain and bran, eyed him suspiciously as he walked up close. The acrid stench of their fresh droppings was thick in the morning air, smelling of fermented grasses and stale oats.

Buck turned away, walked back toward the curving line of the V, then down the creek. At a point some thirty or forty yards downstream, he discovered a small tunnel, just large enough for a man to fit into, burrowed into the hillside. He saw two rust-covered rails jutting out. Two tiny ore cars sat alongside the hole, their wheels shiny, freshly oiled. Tailings that had tumbled down toward the creek were frozen in immobility. He hunched down next to the tunnel, peered inside. It was black as pitch.

"Purdy?"

No answer. The tunnel swallowed up his voice.

Buck stood up and took a sight along the tunnel. If the hole went straight through, it would have an opening on the other side of the hill, along the bottom of the ridge where he had not explored. He retraced his steps and followed the other ridge, back toward the cabin. He peered hard at the ridge, at the space between.

Even so, he almost missed it.

There were no tell-tale tailings. The hole was difficult to see. As he drew close, he saw why. Instead of boring through the hillside, parallel to the lay of the land, the hole went straight down. Its position was blocked from casual view, was invisible from any but the most careful inspection. The ground rose where the shaft was sunk and blended into the ridge from as close as two feet away.

He looked down, saw that this must be the other end of the shaft that had its exit on the creek where he had stood just a few moments before. There were two small rails, the gauge matching the wheels of the tiny ore cars he had seen on the other side. He crawled down the ladder. The hole was narrow. Below, he saw another shaft at right angles to the one leading under the hill. From where he stood, the shaft continued on in the opposite direction. To where? Under Purdy's cabin, he thought. Perhaps as far as to the other side of the V made by the two ridges.

It was pitch dark in the tunnel and just wide enough to allow a single man to enter it. The other shafts were also railed. He had to hunch over to walk down the tunnel. He walked a few feet, became swallowed up in darkness. A wave of claustrophobia swept over him. He backed up, rather than attempt to turn around, wondering if his imagination was not responsible for his difficulty in breathing. He reached the opening, lifted his head up and breathed deeply of the fresh air. He was about to ascend above ground when he heard the sharp clicks of twin hammers cocking.

Buck's blood froze as the metallic sounds grated on his ears.

"Hold her right there, pardner. Don't so much as twitch yore eyelashes or I'll blow ya to kingdom come."

"Purdy?" Bolt squeaked.

"Might be. Might not be. Come up outen that shaft real slow and careful like, pilgrim, or this Greener's li'ble to splatter yore skull all over that hole you're in."

Jess climbed gingerly up the ladder, careful to move slowly, keep both hands in sight.

The old coot had gotten the drop on him for fair and he didn't want a nervous trigger finger stopping all hope of calm conversation between the two. Buck stood up on level ground, faced the two barrels of the shotgun. The old man backed away from him, holding the barrels steady on Buck's midsection. A shot at that range, with both barrels, would cut a man in two.

Moses Purdy looked as if he'd been made out

of twisted cedar and pine. There wasn't a square inch of his flesh that wasn't wrinkled, burned nut brown by the sun. His face looked as though it had been pitchforked atop his head. Straggly grey hair poked from underneath a battered hat that was covered with clay and wet earth, just as were his dingy clothes. His nose appeared to have been broken several times, never in the same place twice. His jaw set off-center, as if it had taken a crack or two, as well.

Jess looked at the man, tried to smile.

The old man looked as if he ate trespassers for breakfast. For all his age, he didn't squint nor quiver. His eyes were clear, black as agate from a dozen feet away. He held the Greener steady as a rock.

Moses Purdy didn't smile. Instead, his mouth pinched up into a hostile pucker, giving him the look of a fighting cock about to pounce.

Buck's smile started to wither on his lips.

"Who be ye and what're ya doin' pokin' in my claim?" Purdy asked tightly.

"Jess Buck, old timer. Came to see you. Called your name a time or two. Thought you might be down working in your mine. If you'll lower that scattergun, I'd like to palaver with you. You're making me mighty nervous and I mean no harm."

"Who told ya 'bout me?"

"Laurie Whiston. At the Palace."

Buck felt the barbed wire in his back tingle. The twin barrels of the shotgun looked like vacant eyes in a skull.

The shotgun lowered several inches.

Purdy tried to smile. The effort merely disassembled his face a little more, shifting the lines around, rearranging the nose. A gag-toothed hole opened just below his nose and one of his cheeks moved out of alignment with the other.

"Laurie Whiston," he cackled. "Why ya oughta have said that in the fust place, pilgrim. She don't give out where my diggins is to jist anybody. Come on over ta the cabin and tell me what's on yore mind."

With relief, Buck walked with Purdy back to the cabin. He noted that the old timer had eased the hammers back down on the shotgun.

"You had me cold back there," Jess said, after they had sat down at a table inside the cabin. "I didn't reckon on miners being so touchy."

Purdy's eyes narrowed, throwing his face out of kilter again.

"Man's got to watch his poke hereabouts. Shady doin's, young 'un. Shady doin's. Techy, you say? Why, hellfire, this's worse'n Hangtown er Cripple Crick. I seed you pokin' around. Laid up fer ye. Ha! Sneaked off like a rabbit, I did, and caught ye down the rabbit hole. But, that ain't no nevermind. What brung ya here to my shack?"

Buck told him.

"And," he concluded, "I was wondering if you could tell me what 'Lost Star' might mean. I'm flat stumped."

Purdy shuffled through his clothes and brought out a small brass box. He snapped it open and snorted a cloud of pale brown snuff. He gagged, spluttered, and shook his head.

"Useta tuck it in my gums," he said. "Teeth started fallin' out and figgered it musta been the snuff. Wanted to go out to Saint Louie and strangle the Garretts personal. Stopped tuckin' it and my teeth kep'a fallin' out, so's I knowed it wasn't the snuff, jest my natural agin'. Now, about that Lost Star Mine. It was Van Duzen found it. Filed on it, some said. Rich. Danged rich ore. Belle, now, that be his daughter. Town over yonder named after that purty little gal, ya know, and wisht ta God more people respected it. She kept mum about that mine. Her man, too. But, I figger Van Duzen found the mother lode."

Purdy's voice had dropped off to an almost reverent whisper when he spoke about the "mother lode." Buck leaned over the table, eager to hear every word.

"You know where the mine was?"

"Near's I know, up Artic Canyon — two, three mile uppards a my diggin's. Few knowed about it at the time, yet talk gits around."

"You mean a lot of people know about the Lost Star?"

Purdy shook his head.

"Not many, but they was always a mystery to it. Confusin' enough? Rightly so, I reckon, but there's another twist to it, young feller. You see they's a couple of Van Duzens. One spells his name different. Now, the other Van Duzen, he had a poke and a half, all right. And his partner kilt him, run off with lots of gold wasn't rightly his'n.

"Yessir, they found Van Duzen dead, and his partner run off down the canyon through Bear Valley and just disappeared. Never seed again. But it was knowed he didn't take all the gold there was, and it was also knowed that he wasn't a real partner of Van Duzen's, but just a worker, sort of, helpin' out. So, everybody figgered Van Duzen's claim could be jumped or taken over since he didn't leave no last will nor testament and didn't have no known kin."

"So, what happened?"

"I checked the filin', and they was no mention of any Lost Star mine. Nobody ever filed a claim on that mine and it twere a pretty rich mine from all that was said and seen."

"So, it's a mystery, then."

"A mystery? You betcha, Buck. A danged big mystery. To this very day. But, I'll allow as I knowed both Van Duzens. Both mighty smart fellers. Both gone now, fer sure. Musta had somethin' though, one or t'other of 'em. Good name fer a mine, too. Lost Star. Yep, it's lost and mebbe it ain't."

"Huh?"

"What say?"

"I'm confused, Purdy. If it wasn't filed on, maybe it was just a rumor. You know, the kind that go through gold fields all the time."

"Heh? Rumor? Yep, mebbe so. Not this'n, though. Too much gold got agoin' down to San Berdoo. Sacks of it. And, the mother lode ain't never been found."

"I thought you said. . . ."

"Oh, that's what I thought. That much gold. Musta been the mother lode. Gold's gotta come from some place, I reckon. Now, you ain't no gold seeker. Least that's what you say and you don't look like no addled prospector. You got took fer yore poke. You 'spectin' to run onto them what took yore gold. You might, too. They got to be the same bunch what's after the Lone Star and everythin' else in this lonesome valley. Wal, they ain't gonna find that mine."

Jess felt the chill bumps rise on his arms, the hackles bristle on the back of his neck.

"Did you know Pentell, the man I shot?" he asked Purdy.

"Knowed who he was. Figgered he was the one who was in on the killin' of Alvin Burriss and Anthony Miller."

"That's the first I've heard of that. You know 'em?"

"Some time back, I had some questions for Burriss and Miller. Burriss 'cause he put me on to the Van Duzen tale in the fust place. And the Miller boy was amarryin' Al's daughter. Figgered they had a claim, same as mine. Moreso, even."

"How so?" asked Buck.

"Burriss told me where to look after Van Duzen was kilt. 'Course they was a lot of talk in the valley back then. Only I listened real hard, tried to sort it out best I could."

"Any idea who killed those two? Was it Pentell? Some others?"

"Might of been. No names never did come up, but I'll bet sovereigns to biscuits it was the same outfit workin' to find the Lone Star and sew up the strings on Holcomb Valley."

"And you don't know who these people are?"

"Nope. Don't make no difference, though. They ain't gonna get claim to that lost mine."

"You seem pretty sure, Purdy."

The old man's nostrils quivered as he worked the snuff into the tiny veins.

"I ought to be sure," he cackled, " 'cause I found it, dangnab it! And, I damn sure filed on it!"

CHAPTER TWELVE

Jess sat stunned for several seconds.

Purdy slapped his knee and cackled like a demented rooster.

Was the man crazy? Buck wondered. He knew the fever that gold brought on a man. It could grip a sane man's mind quicker than lightning and scramble his brains like eggs in a skillet.

Loneliness could add to a man's problems with scrabbling for gold. From the looks of Moses Purdy, he'd been around the Horn a time or two. He didn't appear to have struck it rich, yet, and he wasn't likely to, if past history meant anything. The lone miner seldom earned more than a day's hard wages working by himself. Yet, appearances could be deceiving.

Still, Moses didn't seem to be well off. He was still grubbing underground like a mole. He had few trappings. The loner usually sold out to a sucker before he found the main vein. Discouragement ran rampant in gold camps. Sometimes a man would sell a rich find without realizing he had been close. Capitalists would come in with money raised on shares and bring in expensive mining equipment. They became the millionaires. Not men like Moses Purdy.

"If—if you found the Lost Star, why are you telling me?" Buck asked, deciding to take another tack.

" 'Cause you come recommended. Laurie. She's the only other one what knows. She wouldn't have sent you here 'less'n she wanted me to tell you. Rest of that bunch up here's still lookin' for that Van Duzen mine. Well, I found it and I filed on it."

"The one you're working now?"

"The very same. Looky, that one side there's jist a blind. Place to run the tailin's out. It's the other side what's rich! Goes on and on, no tellin' how fur, right under that other ridge. Found a skeleton buried in that shaft. Cave-in caught him. It's a mine ye can't work in the spring. Too goldarned wet. Gotta watch fer cave-ins. Now, that feller was downright unlucky, wouldn't ye say?"

"Yeah, Purdy," said Buck, drily, "but was he Van Duzen?"

"Who knows? And, if it was Van Duzen, which one? The Van Duzen what's the blacksmith? Nope, not that'n. The Van Deusen what had the rich claim down on Van Duzen crick? Spelled different, e-u-s-e-n, 'stead of u-z-e-n. Don't think so. They found his body in his shack, a .58 caliber hole or two in him. Nope. Twarn't neither of the Van Duzens, less'n there was a third." The old man paused, his eyes twinkling as he looked at the puzzled Buck. "And I heard tell there was."

128

"A third Van Duzen?"

"Could be! Or, mebbe Van Duzen's partner—the one that robbed him. He mighta been the one whose bones was back there in the shaft."

Buck pushed his hat back off his forehead and wiped a streak of sweat off his forehead. The more Purdy talked, the less crazy he seemed. Yet, he presented a puzzling picture. Names were often misspelled in the West. He could see where confusion could occur in the case of the Van Duzens, with a half dozen ways to spell the name, at least: Van Duzen, Van Dusen, Van Deusen, Van Deuzen . . . the variations flowed through his mind until he made a mental note to check the records and mining claims in San Bernardino. There might be some distinction between spellings in some of the records. Besides that, he especially wanted to check the Lost Star. And Purdy.

"Who do you really think was in that shaft, Purdy?"

Purdy got up from the table, then, did a little hop on one foot, shaking his head in silent glee.

"Why, Buck, it's as plain as day! Can't ye figger it?"

"I could try," said Jess. "The Van Duzen in Belleville is still around. He's the blacksmith. The other Van Duzen, who probably spelled his name different, was shot by his partner and robbed. His partner skipped with the gold. Probably changed his name, lit a shuck for parts unknown."

"Right neat, so fur," said Purdy, leaning over the back of the chair he had just vacated. His eyes glittered with excitement, narrowing as he studied Buck more closely. "Go on, go on."

"Now," Buck continued, "everybody heard about Van Duzen's Lost Star mine. But from where? From who? Not from the blacksmith. Maybe from the Van Duzen who was killed. Maybe his claim down the canyon wasn't rich at all. Maybe he carried gold from the Lost Star down to those diggings, just to throw everybody off the track."

"Whoa there, Buck!" Purdy scratched his head, rocked back on his heels. He worried the battered hat on his head until it threatened to fall off. It sat there, cockeyed, while his eyes darkened, widened. "You're a-goin' purty fast for this chile."

Buck suppressed a smile.

If Purdy had meant to confuse him, or pull his leg, he had done him one better. The thought had occurred to him, though, that a man stumbling on a rich claim in crowded quarters might want to divert attention from the true source of his gold. The Van Duzen story was already becoming legend and there was no telling how carefully planned the murder, theft and subsequent search for a lost mine had been. Buck had the feeling, though, that someone mighty smart had engineered the whole thing. There was the matter of the skeleton in the shaft, though. And Purdy himself. How did he know that *this* was the lost mine? And if he had figured it out, why hadn't anyone else?

"Ye done give me pause, young feller. This Van

Duzen was right smart. He coulda done what you said. Kep' his secret to hisself."

"He could have," said Buck. "or, as you said, there could have been another Van Duzen, maybe a brother or an uncle. Father and son. The man you found in the shaft might have been . . ."

Purdy sat down, deadly serious.

"Van Duzen?"

"You said it yourself, once."

"It don't hardly seem possible."

"Listen, Purdy, there's more to it than this. What I'm wondering is why a man like Pentell, knowing he was dying, would mention the name of that mine, the Lost Star. Who was he in with? Who were the others? Do they know you might have found Lost Star? And if they do, maybe you'll wind up in that shaft. . . ."

"Wal, now, I've done plumbed that some meself. You got to help me on that, Buck. Pentell was no miner. Rough bunch he was in with, mighty rough. His kind been comin' to the mountains lately. Driftin' in fer no good reason. You got to look for their main headquarters, see who's a-settin' where they can do the most good. Who aims to stay and who's jest in it fer the gold they can dig up to make 'em feel comfortable."

"If I follow you right, Purdy, you're talking about the Palace. Singleton. Slatter."

"Might be. A couple of snakes. Stayin' put, all right."

Buck had heard enough. He rose from the chair, stuck out his hand. Purdy took it, shook it. The old man had plenty of grip left. He was strong.

"Thanks, Purdy. I'll be seeing you."

"Anytime. You tell Laurie I said howdy. Keep yore mouth tight about this, Buck. I trust ye 'cause Laurie trusts ye."

"I will. Take care, Purdy."

Purdy's eyes bored into Buck's.

"You do the same, pilgrim."

Buck mounted the blue roan, rode to the mouth of the V, rounded the ridge. He looked at the slope carefully, but he was no geologist. If there was gold under the dirt, it was a mystery to him how anybody knew where to look for it, get it out.

Purdy may not have given him the answers, but he had given him more questions. Perhaps that was what he needed just now. Questions demanded answers. The more he looked, the more he was bound to dig up. And, he had a lot of digging to do.

He was grateful for the old prospector for confiding in him. At least he had pointed him in the right direction, even though he took a round-about way to do it. The Palace. That had to be the hub of the illegal activity in Holcomb Valley. But that didn't necessarily mean that Singleton and Slatter were dishonest men. Yet, they were in a perfect spot to find out most of what went on in Belleville, underground. They probably knew something about everything that went on up in these mountains. Pentell had seemed at home at the saloon. There was no proof that he knew Singleton, but the odds were that he probably did.

If Purdy really had found the Lost Star mine, then he was in danger. Pentell had mentioned the mine. That meant that others knew about it too, and were either looking for it, or waiting to jump claim. If they were still looking for it, then Pentell most surely had been one of those searching. And, it was likely that someone had Pentell on his payroll. But who? Had Pentell been trying to tell him a name? Or was that hissing sound he made merely the whisper of his dying breath? It was, Buck believed, a distinct ess sound. Singleton? Slatter? Both of them? Could be.

He would have to keep his eyes open, his ears tuned to pick up further clues.

Something was dead wrong in this valley. He knew that now. Something rotten underneath. And, because he had been robbed, he had unwittingly stumbled onto it. Yet, now that he looked back, it seemed to him that the bandits had known he was coming to Belleville and didn't want him here. Why? Why not just shoot him in the back and be done with it? Unless they wanted him here. Or someone wanted him here. It didn't make sense. Yet this seemed to be their headquarters. The trail led here.

It was a puzzle, all right. Yet Buck aimed to solve it and get his money back, if he could. In this, he realized, he was playing a lone hand.

He followed the creek at a leisurely pace, upstream. It seemed peaceful in the woods, quiet, except for the chatter of squirrels, the raucous screech of jays. Chipmunks scurried underfoot and the creek burbled softly. As he rode, some instinct started gnawing at his senses again. He had learned to pay attention to such feelings. The last time he'd felt the same way, he had been thrown down on and robbed. This time he vowed not to be caught offguard. He turned away from the stream, crossed the road and doubled back, striking out for the shelter of the pine and rock-studded ridge. He dismounted in a sheltered spot, hidden from plain view by a large cedar, some small junipers.

He heard an alien sound, then more noise, movement, somewhere back where he had been, where there should have only been stillness.

Somewhere behind him.

Buck eased his pistol from its holster, thumb on the hammer.

He listened, held his breath.

A Stellar's jay squawked noisily overhead. Buck held perfectly still.

Then, he heard it. The click of a horse's iron hoof on stone. The creak of leather, soft as a whisper.

Buck moved silently behind a tree. The blue roan began to graze. The jay floated away like a blue shadow.

"I lost him," a voice husked. "Where'd he go?"

"Callate, tonto!"

Then, silence again.

Buck strained his ears. He bent down, picked up a small stone in his hand. He threw it toward the creek, several yards from his position.

The stone rattled on the ground, clattered over pebbles, *thunked* into the water.

More movement. Whispering.

Now he knew there were at least two men. He didn't doubt that they were tracking him, ready to bushwhack him. He could almost smell them.

The blue roan snorted.

Buck cursed under his breath.

The silence exploded with the sound of gunfire.

Hooves thundered over hard ground. Loosened rocks rattled. Two riders, shielded by their hats and the trees, streaked toward him. Jess ducked as bullets whistled past his ear, overhead. He sprawled headlong, sprayed by dust and rock chips. Bullets whined near his head and chunks of bark exploded in his face. He twisted, quickly, tried to follow their movement.

He looked up to see the rumps of their horses as the two men sped past.

He recognized one of them.

It was another of the men who had robbed him.

The other, faster, on a fleeter horse, showed him only his back. But, Buck knew who it was.

He half-stood, cocking the Colt in his hand. He fired two quick shots through the trees, trying for a hit. Branches broke off in the path of his bullets. He knew he had missed them clean.

Still, they would know he was alive.

He listened to the crashing of brush, the pounding of hooves receding in the distance. Then, absolute silence.

Buck raced to the roan, took up the reins. There was a bullet crease in the leather of his saddle.

He mounted quickly, reloaded his pistol, shaking out the empty hulls. The men who had ambushed him had gone, probably split up. If he followed them close, they might wait for him, take him easy.

Buck drew breath, forced his blood to stop racing in his veins. He wanted them, wanted them bad, but this was not the time. This was their country, not his. They knew the land, he did not.

The man whose face he had not seen was the fourth man. He was sure of that. The other rider had jingled as he rode past. That was the sound he had first heard. One that he would never forget.

Even though the other man was more elusive, keeping his face hidden, Jess was sure that he was the same one he had glimpsed at a distance down on the desert. A Mexican, perhaps. The way he rode his horse, his clothing, something Indian and secretive about him.

And, something else.

He had heard his voice, speaking in the Spanish tongue. There was a curl to the accent that Buck recognized, from Texas, from his own rides south of the border.

So, the Californio was probably a Mexican.

But, who was he?

Buck didn't know, but he meant to find out.

When he did, he would kill him.

CHAPTER THIRTEEN

The tracks of the two riders faded out near Coyote Flat.

Below, the high desert stretched out in the sun, full of its immense secrets. There was a trail there, dim, untrod since the last rains, and no fresh tracks showed up after a half hour's ride down the slope. He found snubbing posts on the steeper places, so Buck knew that the trail had once been used by wagons coming up from the high desert and descending from the mountains.

He gave up his search, reluctantly, and angled the roan toward Union Flat where he could once again pick up the Gold Fever Trail into Belleville. The last three hours had taught him much about the mountains, had drawn him under their spell. There was a peacefulness here, despite the fact that men with guns were trying to kill him.

He rode his horse boldly up the main street, to the stables, ordered the boy to rub him down and grain him. The roan felt good now that he had spent some time on him.

The stable boy, Kevin Whitaker, a thatch of

straw-colored hair poking out from under his cap, took the fifty-cent piece that Buck pressed into his hand.

"I'll be riding him a lot the next few days," said Jess.

"What's his name?"

"I don't know."

"Horse ought to have a name."

"Well, you name him, then," said Buck. "He was just loaned to me and I might have to give him back."

"I — I'll take good care of him, mister. I heard about you shooting Pentell."

"Best not to talk about that, boy."

"My name's Kevin."

"Kevin. I'll be seeing you."

Buck looked over the other horses in the stable, as a matter of habit, but didn't see any that he recognized. Kevin was already at work, unsaddling the roan in a stall.

Buck didn't go into the saloon, but went straight to his room at the Palace. He failed to see the man in a far corner of the lobby, shielded by a three-week-old newspaper, who watched him cross the lobby and climb the stairs. The man dashed into the saloon as soon as Buck cleared the landing.

Buck's eyes widened when he saw the saddlebags neatly sitting in the center of the bed.

Quickly, he shut the door, locked it.

The saddlebags were not his own, but his heart pounded as he opened one, looked inside. There was his money, in gold and greenbacks. He opened the other one. The same.

He let out a low whistle.

Someone had returned his stolen money!

It appeared, after a hasty count, that the entire $8000 was there. Puzzled, Buck hefted the saddlebags, slung them over his shoulder. He didn't want to risk having that much money in his room. He knew it would be best if he rode to San Bernardino, found a reliable bank where he could deposit the greenbacks, cash in the gold.

No sooner had he made up his mind, than he was startled by a resounding knock on his door.

"Open up in there, Buck. It's Dobbs."

Dobbs! What could he want?

It was just too pat. The money. Dobbs.

Somebody had set him up!

"Just a minute, Dobbs," Buck said, heading toward the open window. It was fifteen feet to the ground.

"Open up or we'll break the door down, dammit!"

Jess didn't wait to see if Dobbs would follow through on his threat. He climbed over the sill, dropped to the ground. Pain shot up through his boot heels, made his shins go numb.

Behind him, he heard a crash, the sound of splintering wood, angry shouts. Clutching the saddlebags, he raced on wobbly heels toward the stables. He knew it wouldn't take long for Dobbs and his Vigilantes to alert the whole town, the valley, even.

Somebody had boxed him in, for sure.

With hot-tempered men like Dobbs, he realized he would have little chance of explaining his side of the story. Worse, he couldn't count on anyone in Holcomb Valley for help.

It must have been Singleton who set him up, he realized. Someone who had access to the room, no questions asked. Singleton, or Slatter. Same thing. If so, then Singleton must know the men who robbed him. It was a sobering thought.

Slatter, too, had to be in on it. He worked for Singleton. Maybe he was one of the same bunch. Maybe they all worked for Singleton.

These thoughts tumbled through his mind as he hobbled to the stables, the pain in his shins and heels diminishing somewhat. He went in the back way.

"Need my horse fast," he said to Whitaker. "Get my blanket and saddle."

Kevin looked at him, startled, a pitchfork in his hand. He opened his mouth to say something, but only a squeak came out.

Instead, a man stepped out of one of the stalls, a sawed-off shotgun leveled at Buck's belly.

"You won't be needin' no horse, Buck," said the man.

Percy Jense. His eyes were cold on Buck's. Kevin stood frozen in mid-stance, his pitchfork suspended empty in the air.

Buck weighed his chances. If they took him now, he'd hang before sundown. Jensen's look told him that. His eyes said "rope" and his scattergun emphasized that chilling point.

Dobbs and his bunch were rope happy, apparently, as evidenced by the four men they had strung up when he first arrived in Holcomb. Some of those men might even have been guilty as charged. But, Buck damned sure wasn't guilty of anything and he had no wish to dance on the end of a lariat to suit Dobbs' blood lust.

Seconds slipped by and Jensen's hands began to tremble. A bad sign. Buck sensed that Jensen, being alone, wasn't too sure of himself. He didn't have the "mob" behind him. The man might decide to shoot him without the formality of a hearing, much less a trial. Buck knew that he'd have to act or throw up his hands and let Jensen take him. He glanced at Whitaker, who was standing slightly behind Jensen and off to the side.

Buck made a quick decision. Whitaker was out of the line of fire, but that condition might not continue to exist. Everything would depend on Buck's timing, his own speed with the six-gun.

He decided to take the chance.

"Throw your pitchfork into him, kid!" Buck yelled, looking in Kevin's direction.

Jensen twisted his head, started to turn. The shotgun swung away from Buck for a split-second.

Too late, Jensen realized his mistake.

Buck cleared leather before Jensen could recover. Kevin remained frozen, powerless to move. Jensen's mouth dropped open as Buck hammered back and triggered a shot before Jensen could swing the scattergun back. The roar of burnt powder filled the air with sound. White smoke and flame belched from the barrel of Buck's Colt. The bullet caught Jensen in the side, just below the armpit.

The soft lead flattened, exploded against a rib, splinted, hammered through muscle to Jensen's heart. The pumping muscle took the shock, quivered, and began beating wildly out of control. Blood gushed from an artery, vessels, as the expanded slug smashed through lung and cartilage.

Jensen staggered sideways; his reflexes setting off both hammers of the shotgun. The double ought pellets ripped harmlessly into a clump of stacked hay.

Kevin yelled a meaningless cry.

"Sorry, kid," muttered Buck, dashing for the hanging tack. He holstered his Colt, grabbed a bridle off the wall. He wrestled it onto the blue roan and fastened the buckles. He led the animal out back as Kevin stood there, shivering in fear and bewilderment.

There was no time to saddle the horse. Buck threw the saddle bags on the roan's back, swung up atop them. He rode out, sitting atop the bags, ducking down as he booted the horse's flanks. He leaned over the horse's withers, Indian style. He didn't want to get shot in the back when he was so close to freedom.

He heard men shouting. A rifle boomed. Buck heard the ball whistle wide of his path, but the sizzle sent a chill up his spine. Another rifle boomed and a bullet whined over his head like an angry hornet. He rode through the town, reined over hard to avoid an arrestre. Miners, still working, scattered and dove into placer ditches as he rode past, zig-zagging the roan. He dodged placer troughs and leaped the horse over diggings. Bullets whizzed overhead and wide of their mark.

The general confusion helped him in his escape.

The roan laid back its ears and ran. Ran like the wind. Ran hard away from the men on foot shooting wildly into the air. Buck hugged the horse's back, lying out flat as he could and gave the animal its head.

Soon, he left the shouts and the din behind him. He cleared the wide meadow and climbed into the rocks, heading deeper into the pine, the oak, the cedar and juniper that grew thick beyond the wide swath of valley that was the site of Belleville. He crossed Holcomb Creek at a wild gallop, climbed still higher, until his breath caught in his chest and his side ached as if he had been stabbed.

He brought the roan up when he heard the wheeze begin in its chest. He held horse steady while he listened, caught his breath. His blood raced and his heart hammered in his chest like a stamp mill. Sweat drenched his flesh, soaked through his clothes. He slid his hat off his head, wiped the sweat band dry. Heaving for breath, he drew his pistol, ejected the empty hull. He fingered a bullet from his gunbelt, rammed it into the cylinder. He looked over his shoulder and listened.

It was quiet.

He rested for five minutes until his breathing returned to normal. He patted the roan on the neck, spoke a few words to the horse.

There were mounds all around him. He knew he was in a burial ground. Sacred to the Serranos who had summered in these high places before they were wiped out by the soldiers, the white men. He shivered as the sweat on his body cooled him down.

He clucked to the roan, moved out slow. He walked the horse for twenty minutes until the animal cooled down, breathed well again.

He cut another path, stopped again, ten minutes later.

Listened.

He rode on again, through thick trees, over rocks, past a wide cut. He found a game trail that led to another trail that widened, showed signs of travel. He looked at the sky, saw he was heading west and south.

No one had followed him this far.

There was utter stillness about him.

After the noise in Belleville, it was almost spooky, this silence.

His gunbelt was empty.

His sixgun was full.

And, he had his money back, a good horse under him.

Buck drew a deep breath, assessed his situation.

He was alive, had money. In San Bernardino, he could buy a saddle, a spare pistol, a rifle, another horse, new clothes. There, too, he could do the checking he had to do.

His enemies would not be looking for him

down in the flatland. Not that far away. Not right away. If he moved fast, he could take care of his business, be back in the valley before the word reached the lower settlements. If necessary, he could bring provisions, camp out in the woods until he found the answers he needed.

Buck knew that the old Mormon Trail went through the Cajon Pass to San Bernardino. He could not turn back, take the short cut down the creek trail. It would be quicker and safer to keep heading toward the pass, drop down out of the mountains there. All he had to do was find a trail leading that way. He figured he was bound to cut one if he angled to the southwest. If he hurried, he could reach San Bernardino sometime that same night. That would be to his advantage. Fewer people would be apt to notice him. He could find a quiet place to stay, go to the bank in the morning, take care of business. With luck, he would be gone by the following night, riding a fresh horse with a new rig, wearing new clothes.

A half hour later, Buck cut a well-worn trail that seemed to head in the general direction of Cajon Pass. The trail kept widening and showed signs of heavy, recent travel. He wondered why such a trail would be where it was. It was not on one of the regular supply routes. The trail was too rugged, too far from the other main routes. The Mormon Trail led north to Victor, south to San Bernardino. But there was no need to pick up the trail from Holcomb Valley. there were easier routes to both places.

Whoever used this trail, used it for purposes

other than honest ones.

Curious, Buck began scanning the ground for separate tracks, ones not blended in with the others. Finally, he isolated some tracks, stopped the roan, dismounted and examined them more carefully. He walked on, leading the horse, seeing other hoof prints. He studied them, memorized them.

He stood up, after seeing one set of tracks and whistled inaudibly.

The tracks were no more than a few hours old. They came into the trail from a point that indicated the riders had come from the direction of Coyote Flat. The tracks were those of the two horses he had encountered that morning, when their riders had ambushed him.

The men who had shot at him, robbed him previously, had come this way—and not more than a hour or so before!

He mounted up again, rode on with fresh purpose. Although he was not prepared to meet the bandits in combat just yet, he would be soon. Now that he knew one of their escape routes, he could return and track them down or wait them out.

It seemed even more important, now, that he continue on to San Bernardino and reoutfit there. If the trail he now followed came out on the Cajon Pass, between the toll house and San Bernardino, then he would know one more thing about the outlaws who had robbed him.

The puzzle was becoming more complicated, but he was getting more pieces to help him solve it.

Later, he emerged above the pass, his suspicions confirmed.

He looked back at the point where he had ridden out of the high country, started his descent. The trail was invisible from the Mormon Trail.

Buck had a hunch he would find more pieces to the puzzle in San Bernardino.

He rode through the pass, making good time. He passed a freighter and four mules, waved and rode on. Dusk caught up with him at Little Mountain. He came to the Base Line, rode east as darkness settled over the valley that had once been one huge rancho.

His timing, he thought, could not have been better.

CHAPTER FOURTEEN

Bert Singleton paced the floor of his office, striding through clouds of cigar smoke.

His boots creaked on the wood flooring, his weight straining the boards. His face was flushed with anger. His eyes crackled as he looked at each man in the room, men who avoided looking at him.

Vern Slatter sprawled in a chair, puffing on his own cigar. Randy Falconer twitched nervously on a divan, glancing sidelong at Earl Dobbs, who sat next to him. Dobbs was also smoking. The air was foul with sweat and smoke and strong words.

"Dammitall, Dobbs, you let Buck slip right through your fingers. The man's a thief. Robbed me of eight thousand dollars."

"I know, Bert, I know. We thought he'd — I mean, well, I thought he'd open his door or stay there till we busted it down."

"You thought," sneered Singleton, halting in front of the corpulent Dobbs. "Hell, you brag about being a vigilante and you can't even catch a man dead to rights. Buck had my cash in his paws and you let him get away. Now, he's gone to god knows where!"

Falconer, a thin, twidgety man in his forties, raised his eyes to focus on Singleton. Falconer wore his hair parted down the middle, slicked down and back so that his forehead looked wide and shiny above his thin hooked nose. He coughed and stood up.

"Mister Singleton, we didn't know that this man Buck had the money. I mean, you say you were robbed, but . . ."

"But nothing," interrupted Singleton. "Isn't my word good enough in this town?"

"Yes, I suppose so, but evidence . . . I mean we were really over-riding our authority in this instance."

"Bull," interjected Slatter, half-lidded eyes peering at Falconer disdainfully. "This Buck's a known outlaw. Been running stolen horses from border to border. He's a gunman with a reputation that stretches from here to the Brazos."

"Your sayso Mister Slatter?" asked Falconer, his thin eyebrows arching into dark bows.

Slatter's eyes narrowed to indignant slits.

"Mine and Mister Singleton's. We saw the man sneakin' outa here with the cash box receipts. In his saddlebags."

"Now, now, gentlemen, there's no need to argue all night," Dobbs said. "It was my, ah, job to apprehend this Buck. First time I ever laid eyes on him I knew he was a hardcase, fit only for a rope. I let him get away and he escaped justice—but only for a time. We, ah, that is, I, will get him."

Singleton looked at Dobbs with a glare of contempt.

"Dobbs," he said, "I hope you can back up what you say. I'm out eight thousand in gold and greenbacks. If that isn't enough for you, he's guilty of murder—Jensen, poor bastard. You find Buck and get my money back. The next time I see him he'd better be swinging on that juniper outside."

Dobbs knew he had been dismissed. He rose up from his seat and offered his hand to Singleton. Bert turned away from the chubby man and went behind his desk. Slatter turned away, not so much embarrassed for Dobbs, as disgusted. Randy Falconer reached the door first. He opened it, then turned to face Singleton's disdainful back. Sounds of the saloon below drifted into the office room.

"If we get this Buck, Mister Singleton," said Falconer, "we'll listen to his side of the story too. There is probably more here than meets the eye."

Singleton's back stiffened, but he did not turn around.

Falconer and Dobbs went out, leaving the door open.

"Shut that door, Vern."

Slatter relit his cigar, closed the door. Puffs of smoke billowed from his mouth, ragged at his eyes.

"That suckegg, Dobbs," Singleton snarled, turning to face Slatter. "He botched it."

"By now, Buck shoulda been just another cottonwood blossom. So now, what, Bert?"

"Where you figure Buck headed?"

"The Pueblo maybe. Or San Bernardino. Hell, he could of gone anywheres."

"He could have," Singleton said thoughtfully, pooching out his lips. "He's got his cash back. But, there's something about that man that bothers me. He doesn't run true to any pattern. First of all, the boys made a mistake in not killing him in the first place. I know, they got jumped and thought he'd die natural out there in the desert. But he didn't.

"Second, he's snooping around here too fast to suit me. The way he took down Pentell worries me, too. Pentell was fast, mighty fast. Almost as fast as you, Vern. And, he slipped away from Dobbs and Falconer, rubbed out Jensen slicker'n calf shit on a prod-pole. Now, Jensen was a nervous sort, but a mean bearcat if I ever saw one. He didn't flinch at blood or a stretched neck. According to the Whitaker kid, Jensen had the drop on Buck. By rights, he should have cut the bastard in two with that scattergun. So, what happens? Buck drops him like a poleaxed steer."

"Lucky," said Slatter.

"Lucky, my ass."

"What're you getting at, Bert?"

"I think Buck will be back. He came here for a reason — was coming here before the boys took his poke. My hunch is he's down in San Bernardino right this minute, up to no good. Maybe set on getting outfitted to do some hard work up here. When he comes back, he'll be on the prod, with blood in his eye. He's dangerous, but he'll be more dangerous now that he knows he's been set up. Ain't nothin' so wily as a fox that's gotten out of the trap."

"So, what do we do, then?"

"Box him in good. Fix it so he can't get out of the next loop we throw."

Slatter walked over to the desk and ground out his cigar in a brass ashtray.

"How ya figger doin' that?"

Singleton went to the sideboard and pulled out a bottle of *aguardiente*. He poured two glasses full, gave one to Slatter.

Slatter downed the brandy in a single gulp. His eyes watered, but held their steady focus. He didn't even smack his lips. Singleton sipped his drink, wondered how Slatter even stayed on his feet drinking that way.

"Slatter, we've got to get the Valley turned against Buck. We already have ammunition from the robbery set-up. Be hell getting any sympathy for Jensen, but we might be able to swing it."

"Falconer smells a rat."

"To hell with Falconer! That's why we've got to bolster the charges against Buck. Get the miners against him and he won't be able to move four feet in any direction either in Bear Valley or Holcomb without getting a pick buried in his skull."

"Pretty ornery bunch, them miners. Don't see how you figger to set them against Buck. They'll put up with a lot, same as a mule."

"Yeah, a lot, but not too much. Just ask yourself something, Vern. Which miner has the respect of all of them? Which miner is looked up to because he's been around, minds his own business, yet helps out anybody who hits him up for a stake?"

"You mean Moses Purdy?"

Singleton cracked a sly smile, took another sip of his brandy.

"Right, Vern. Moses Purdy."

Slatter felt the hackles rise on the back of his neck as Singleton stared at him, hard-eyed.

"You mean . . .? Bert, I — I don't know. Maybe you better check with your partner. I reckon . . ."

"Shut up!" snapped Singleton. "I told you never to mention that. To anyone! Not even me."

"Hell, Bert, dammitall, you're making war smoke here and I just don't know. Old Purdy, hell, he's pert near a — a landmark in these parts."

"That's just the idea, Vern," Singleton said tightly, "you got to kill Purdy and lay the blame on Buck." He paused, looked up at the ceiling. When he resumed talking, his voice was lazy with musing aloud. "Should be easy to do. We know Buck was out at Purdy's place this morning. The old geezer hasn't been to town since then. Yeah, it could be done. Easy. Make it look like Buck did him in."

"Jesus, Bert. How?"

Singleton walked to the window, looked out over the wide meadow in back of the Palace. Looked out at the darkness, the moon-silvered grasses, the amber light of lamps and lanterns in cabin windows.

"We've got some of Buck's papers that were in

his saddlebags along with the money. We've got his horse. It won't be hard."

Slatter considered what Singleton had said.

"It might work," he said, finally.

"Damned right it will work. Vernon, you do this right and you won't have any worries about your future with me. It won't be long until everything falls right into my lap. Now, get to it. Alone. Don't take anybody with you. This'll be just between you and me."

Slatter nodded, but he started to shake his head involuntarily. Something was wrong, but he couldn't put his finger on it. Something inside him got cold in a hurry and the room started to get small, close in on him.

Singleton walked to the safe, spun the dial. He ran through the combination, cracked the bar. The safe door spun open. He reached inside, riffled through a cigar box and pulled out a sheaf of wrinkled papers. He handed them to Slatter.

"These are bills of sale with Jess Buck's name on them, his signature. Leave a couple in Purdy's hands after you shoot him. Shoot him dead and the hardest way you can. Work him over. Use a Colt, one of those converted ones if you can. A forty-five ball. That's what Buck carries and what he killed Pentell and Jensen with."

"I saw it, the bastard. Man with a pistol like that can walk all over cap'n ball."

"Ball don't know what brand gun it come out of. I got a Remington convert forty-five works pretty fair."

"Make it look like Purdy had a hard time

154

dying. We've got to stir up the miners in a big way."

Singleton's savage smile sent chills up Slatter's spine.

He was used to doing jobs for Bert, but never anything like this. Still, money was money. It didn't matter much how a man got it.

Slatter took the papers from Singleton, looked them over.

"This ain't a daytime job, Bert."

"No."

"We ever get caught. . . ." Slatter slashed a finger across his throat, made a sound: *geek*.

"You do it, Vern, and I'll make it right with you."

"Um."

Slatter stuffed the slips of paper into his pocket, put on his hat, squared it up on his head.

Just then, they both heard a scraping sound at the door.

"What was that?" Slatter asked.

"I don't know," said Singleton, in hushed, sepulchral tones. He strode to the door, snatched it open. He stared over the balcony, down the stairs, across the part of the saloon he could see.

"Damn!" he exclaimed.

Slatter came up behind him, stood on tiptoe to peer over Singleton's shoulder.

A man hit the bottom of the stairs, threaded his way through the crowd.

"Too late to stop him," said Singleton, more to himself than to Slatter.

"Yeah. People might wonder."

"And put two and two together."

"Never figured him to a turncoat," mused Vern, shaking his head.

"The sneaky bastard," muttered Singleton.

Slatter drew a breath, came back down on his heels. He walked away from the doorway.

He now had something else to worry about.

"Bert, he's going to be trouble."

"He's already trouble, Vern. You'll have to take him down, too."

Slatter tensed, spun on one heel to face his boss. His eyes seemed shadowed from knuckled brows. His mouth was tight at the corners, his jaw sharp as an axe blade.

"You want me to start writin' down a list?"

"I'm in no mood for funny talk, Vern."

"Christ, Bert. You take a man down face to face, it's hard enough. But you shoot rabbits, another thing. Purdy. I'm goin' to see his face a long time and be lookin' over my shoulder a long time."

Singleton shrugged. His eyes turned vacant as coins put on a dead man's lids.

The gunman puckered his lips in thought.

He wanted to say something, but knew now that it would do no good. He had never thought much about mortality, but now he did. His belly turned queasy and he wanted to either hit someone or walk way. He thought of the alternatives, and he thought about how good he had it now.

Singleton turned away from him as if reading Slatter's thoughts.

"Better get going on those things, Vern," said

Singleton, quietly dismissing his hired gun.

Slatter said nothing. In a moment, he was gone.

Singleton closed the door of his office, locked it.

He felt a tightness in his chest, a band encircling his head. Things were happening fast too to suit him. Things he could not control. If he didn't pull them all together quick, every plan he had made would blow up on him.

"Damn," he said, to no one.

The man who had been listening outside the door had been Randy Falconer.

A trusted man, once.

Now, Singleton wondered just who could trusted.

Randy couldn't. Nor could he be allowed to live with the information he had.

Well, Slatter would take care of that, too.

After a few minutes, Singleton took a fresh cigar out of the humidor on his desk, bit off the end. He stuck it in his mouth, did not light it. He drew himself up, forced a smile before he opened his door, walked out on the balcony. He turned, locked the door.

Then, he started for the stairs, summoning up a smile on his face.

He smiled, he slapped a few men on their backs, but he was in a hurry. A real hurry.

There was someone he had to see right away.

CHAPTER FIFTEEN

Judge W.D. Frazee opened the door. The knocking had been insistent.

"Yes," he blinked, "what is it?"

"Mornin'," said a voice.

Frazee's eyes focused on two men. One was a friend, the other unknown to him.

The judge attempted a smile.

"Billy. Billy Holcomb. Come on in. Why didn't you say it was you? What time is it?"

Holcomb laughed.

The sun was a buttery disk behind morning haze from the valley. It was no longer early and once the mist burned off it was going to be hotter than the hinges of hell.

Holcomb, a lean, short man with windburned face, slender hands, smiled sheepishly. "Urgent business, Judge. Wanted to talk to you before you left home. This here gentleman's Jess Buck.

The judge blinked again.

Jess smiled thinly, shifted the saddlebags in his hand.

"Buck?"

Holcomb stepped brightly past Frazee, motioned for Buck to follow. Inside, he pushed the door gently shut.

"The man I told you about, Walter. Come in from Tucson. Been in Belleville."

Frazee stared blankly for a moment, then nodded energetically.

"Yes, yes, the man. Pleased to meet you, Mister Buck," said the judge cordially. "Come, come, we must talk." He led the two men into his combination parlor and study. The three of them clacked through a beaded portiere. Frazee waved them to comfortable leather chairs. He sat in a wing-backed chair that made him appear smaller in stature than he actually was.

"Sarah's not up yet," Frazee apologized, "or I'd offer you coffee."

"That's all right, Judge," said Buck. "We won't be long." He let the saddlebags in his hand drop to the floor.

"It worked," said Holcomb. "They took the bait. Better'n we expected."

"That so, Buck?"

"Here's the money taken, to the penny. Different saddlebags."

"Tell me everything," said Frazee, stroking his mutton-chop sideburns. He peered at Buck closely with clear hazel eyes.

Buck told him the same story he had told Billy Holcomb, now the Constable in San Bernardino, earlier that day at Holcomb's house. Nancy, Billy's wife, had served them coffee and breakfast. Frazee slid to the edge of his chair, listened intently.

"Here," said Buck, handing the judge several papers, "are receipts duly signed by the Wells Fargo man in Tucson for horses and wagons sold. These are bills of sale for the horses, bought in the Pueblo of Los Angeles. This money here in the saddlebags represents several such sales, all legal, all duly noted and witnessed."

"We're turning everything over to the prosecuting attorney as evidence," said Holcomb.

"Fine, fine. You did just fine," said Frazee. "But you still have to locate the men we're after. . . ."

"I do," said Buck. "But I thought I'd better turn this over to Billy before I go back up. I never expected they'd try to hang me for stealing my own money."

"Yes. You say Dobbs was one of them?"

"He's the apparent head of the vigilantes."

"Proof?"

"Eye-witness testimony," said Buck. "I recognized his voice outside my door when he came after me."

"We need the names of all of them. And who's behind them. Dobbs has about as much spine as a lizard."

"True," said Buck.

"Walt, it's time to give Buck the authority we promised him," said Holcomb quietly.

"A bit early, isn't it?" said Frazee.

"Yes," said Buck. "I'm not going to come out in the open, but I want to work officially now."

"I see," said Frazee. "Billy?"

"I'm ready to swear him in, Walter. I'm tied up in San Bernardino right now. Buck has gotten further on this than anyone else."

Frazee got up, fully primed for the day now.

"So be it," he said. "Gentlemen, I'll be with you in a quarter hour."

Billy looked at Buck after the judge left the room.

"Jess, this isn't going to make it any easier. If Singleton's tied in to this outfit, you got real trouble."

"I know, Billy. We never said it would be easy, did we? I owe you this favor."

"You've wiped out any debt to me a long time ago, Jess."

Buck took in a breath. Maybe. But not the way he looked at it. A year ago, three men had robbed the San Bernardino Land Bank, gotten away clean. They split up, kept the money hidden. The men were all working cowmen. They wore kerchiefs over their faces during the robbery. Officials were stumped. Buck worked with one of the men, had his suspicions. He began keeping an eye out on the man, following him when he went to town, checking out who came to see him. One of the man's frequent visitors was a deputy sheriff from San Bernardino.

Buck finally put it together, realizing that the deputy had set up the bank job and was keeping the robbers informed of the investigation's progress.

Buck found the hidden money, was taking it to San Bernardino when he was jumped by the four men. At that time, Holcomb and several deputies appeared, saved Buck's life. They had, at first, thought Buck was in cahoots with the robbers, but Holcomb had been the first to realize that Buck was doing a better job tracking the robbers than any one else. He was the only one, however, who believed Buck was an honest man. He offered Buck a job on the spot, which Buck refused.

But, one day, a large herd of horses had been rustled and a friend of Buck's killed. He went to Holcomb and learned that the authorities were stumped on who the rustlers were, but that all trails led to the valley named after the Constable. Billy made Buck another offer. This time, because a friend had been killed savagely, he took it, went undercover for nearly a half a year.

In fifteen minutes, Frazee was back, dressed for town. The three men rode to Court Street.

An hour later, after turning over the money and papers to the prosecuting attorney, Buck was sworn in as a Special Deputy, given papers of jurisdiction and authority. Judge Frazee pinned on the badge. Buck took it off, put it in his pocket. Holcomb and Frazee shook Buck's hand.

"You're getting close, Jess."

"I know, Billy."

"Don't let them. . . ."

"I won't," said Buck. "This business will stay just between us for a while?"

"For a while. I'm giving you a free hand up there."

"I know. I appreciate it, Billy."

Buck spent the next two hours outfitting himself. He bought himself a new mount, saddle, saddlebags, a good mountain rifle, powder, ball, provisions.

Finished with that business, he returned to the Court House where he asked to see certain records. He poured over abstracts, transfers, grant deeds, quitclaims, a multitude of mining claims, sorting them out. He formed a picture in his mind of the land titles and mining claims that bobbed up here and there like corks in a rain barrel.

He checked every name that he had run across in Holcomb Valley, including Jensen, Pentell, Dobbs, Foster, Singleton, Slatter, Machado, Purdy and Whiston.

There were several surprises that made his skin prickle.

Satisfied that he had learned all that he could, Buck stopped for lunch at El Rancho Cafe, a wayside saloon and eatery that catered to travelers and locals, newly built on Waterman Road. He ordered a drink of whiskey from the bar and drank it neat, then went to a table. A Mexican waiter took his order for beefsteak, beans, tortillas and beer. He sipped on the beer and looked around. There were few patrons there, that late in the day, and he knew none of them. His mind sorted through the maze of recent events. He knew he faced many obstacles upon his return to Holcomb Valley and Belleville. But, he felt he had made great strides toward finding the answers he sought.

He planned to use Kevin Whitaker as a witness in order to clear himself in the shooting of Jensen. He wanted to talk to Moses Purdy again and tell him what he had found out concerning the mining claims.

Purdy had been right about Van Duzen, or Van Dusen, Van Deusen, et al. No one by any one of those names had filed a claim on a Lost Star mine. There had been no such listing in the records. Jed Van Dusen was a blacksmith, whose daughter, Belle, had provided the name for Belleville. A Van Duzen had filed a claim on the creek that ran between Holcomb and Bear Valley. No one with the spelling of Van Deusen had filed on any land in San Bernardino County.

There was, however, another puzzling fact that Buck had turned up, or failed to turn up. Moses Purdy had not filed on his claim, either.

Buck wondered why. The claim seemed to be pretty well set up, worked. The rails, the ore cars, though small, indicated an operation that was promising, if not paying. There were not many lone hardrock miners up in Holcomb. Most of the miners were placer men, panners. The big outfits could afford to follow a vein, but not the pick and shovel men. Yet Purdy's mine was deep, far-reaching, tunnels blasted through solid rock.

Someone had evidently put a lot of time in on that mine. But who? Purdy? Someone else? Maybe.

Not likely, though. The mine was difficult to locate. Even if one knew the general location, he would still have to stumble right on it, to find it.

On the creek side, it was easier to spot, but even there, the earth showed signs of being cleared up as if someone wanted to leave as few traces of mining activity as possible.

But Purdy hadn't been working that hill. He was obviously working the shaft that went in the opposite direction. Maybe he had found a lode so hot he didn't want to stake it out. Maybe Moses Purdy was playing a cagey game of hide-and-seek. Close to the vest. Poor-mouthing it when he really had stumbled on to a rich claim.

Some of the oldtimers were like that, Buck knew. Purdy had been around. That much showed. In his own way, he was a pretty shrewd old codger. He'd no doubt seen a lot of his friends go under. Claim jumpers. Bandits. Sharp operators. Such types would have taken their toll among miners in that region, elsewhere. So, a man like Purdy would be a cautious man, even a suspicious one. Then why hadn't he filed on his claim?

Buck didn't have a clue.

Acting on a hunch, Buck had filed on the claim himself, under two names. His and Purdy's. If Purdy got angry about it, well, he couldn't help that. He had, in fact, filled out a quitclaim deed so that the claim was really all in Purdy's name. If anything turned up, Purdy would be protected, despite himself. But, now, the claim would be public knowledge, if anyone wanted to dig. And Buck figured it might smoke somebody out into the open. If Purdy said anything, Buck would just hand him the quitclaim and Purdy could file that anytime he wanted.

It was risky, bringing the claim out in the open this way, but if Buck's hunch proved correct, someone would move in on Purdy, in a hurry. No matter. He would defend Purdy's claim should others move to take it from him. Buck was counting on Purdy's eventual acceptance of his move, since he could explain to the old man that he was leaving himself wide open without a bonafide claim to the mine. If the mine proved out, well, so much the better. Purdy might even thank him.

The waiter brought the food, set it down noisily in front of Buck.

"I'll have another *cerveza* and a copy of *The Guardian* if you have it," he said.

"We have it," said the waiter, a chunky man in his forties. "One moment."

Buck spooned the chili-laced *salsa casera* over his steak, smeared butter on a tortilla, filled it with beans and rolled it up like a diminutive rug. The waiter brought the beer and newspaper. Jess read while he ate, keeping one ear open to the sounds inside and outside the cafe.

The door opened and a man came into the cafe, spurs jingling, boots pounding on the floor.

Jess looked up, startled.

Then, his eyes widened as he realized that he knew the man. The other spotted him at the same time.

"Well, I'll be! Jess Buck! If you ain't a sight for sore eyes!"

Buck dropped a forkful of steak back to the plate.

"Dal Nickson? Damned right. Come on over, hoss, set."

Nickson strode to the table. His legs were bowed from years in the saddle. His ruddy face was as much windburned as whiskeyed, and his blue eyes crackled in deep-set sockets framed by wrinkles. He was just under six feet, with a belled nose, small, thin-lipped mouth that was chapped and cracked. His clothes were dusty and the kerchief around his neck was drenched with sweat.

"Heard tell of you in Tucson, Jess," Nickson said, as he sat down. "Boy, bring us a couple of those glasses and yore best drinkin' likker," he yelled to the passing *mozo*. "Said as how you'd be in these parts, forkin' a fresh horse. Yair, they done tole me what happened. I brung in a herd of beef for Rancho Cucamonga, come back thisaway to look you up."

"Who'd you talk to?"

"Billy Edwards. Nick Tanner."

"That so? They back in Tucson?"

"Seems like."

Nickson waited to hear everything and Buck told him, mainly to keep him from talking so much. Nickson liked gossip as much as he did cattle. But, when the chips were down, he was a man who wouldn't back away. He had ten or twelve years on Buck.

When Jess finished his story, Nickson looked him square in the eyes.

"Looks like you need some help, Jess. I ain't doin' much at the moment."

"It's a big chunk to bite, Dal."

"I got good teeth."

"You're buying into a cold deck. Lots of jokers.

Dal laughed heartily.

"Hey, Jess, I'm at loose ends. You're gonna get a herd together one of these days, if I know you, and I wanna side you in this."

Buck looked at his friend. Some of the laugh lines in Dal's face were hardening into baked arroyos. The blood vessels in his hands stood out blue in the harsh light of afternoon. The whites of his eyes were smoking with the dust of too many trails. Maybe it was time that Dal settled down, quit chasing the back ends of horses all over creation. Yet, Buck wasn't ready for him yet. This was a new and dangerous trail.

"Don't turn me down, Jess," Dal said, low, as if reading Buck's thoughts.

"All right, Dal. Hungry?"

"Nope. I ate downtown. I'm ready when you are."

Buck shoved *The Guardian* aside. The date on it was July 3, 1864.

As Buck was paying up, a man came into The Rancho, no more than a boy, really. He was out of breath, wide-eyed. He went up to the bar, not looking to either side of him.

"Hey, Ken," he said to the bartender, "there's been a murder up in Holcomb."

"So, what else is new, Balcom?"

"Well, it was this old miner, see, and everyone's shapin' ropes over it. Some Texican's sposed to have done it. They're after his hide."

"Who had his lamp blown out?" asked Ken

Elves, handing the boy a pail of beer.

"Some old geezer name of Purdy. Moses Purdy."

Jess Buck stiffened.

Dal Nickson looked at his friend and his eyes dimmed with concern.

"And what was that Texican's name?" asked Elves.

"Buck something."

"Never heard of him," said the bartender.

"Come on, Dal," said Buck, "the fat's in the fire. Let's ride."

CHAPTER SIXTEEN

Amy Foster looked at her father, a look of defiance raging on her features.

"I don't care what they say. I don't believe it. That man may be a lot of things, but he's not a cold-blooded murderer."

"Nevertheless, Amy," said Foster, "the evidence shows otherwise. Moses Purdy was brutally shot dead. He was unarmed. His hands were clutching papers with Buck's name on them, his signature. As if he wanted to name his killer."

Her father sat in the large easy chair, his legs stretched out, his boots tilting at an angle on the hardwood floor. Lamplight warmed the room although it was just past dusk. Dark came to the mountains early and left the valley dark before the sun had actually set over the Pacific Ocean.

Amy stood at the hearth, just outside the lampglow, her eyes flashing. The livingroom smelled of wood and leather, the faint scent of lamp oil.

"That's just it, Father," she said vehemently. "Somebody made it look like that! If Jess Buck killed Moses, would he leave those papers behind?"

"You've got a point, Amy. Not much of one, but a point. Still, if Buck didn't do it, who did? Why?"

"I don't know. But we should try to find out. We should help the man."

"Look, he's already accused of stealing eight thousand dollars from Bert. The man's a gunman. He admits it. Nobody knows why he came to Holcomb, nor where he's from, really. Texas, they say, but that's a long way from here. Somebody saw him go up to Purdy's place the other day. What was he doing there?

"I haven't seen Bert, but he'll probably stop by," Amy said wryly. "We can listen to what he has to say about that robbery. I don't for a minute feel the man you talked to the other day, who turned down your job offer, would steal or shoot down an unarmed old man."

"So now you're a judge of character?"

"Why not?"

"Women!" Foster snorted. "All sentiment and intuition. No logic."

"You wouldn't say that if Mother were alive. You always said she was smarter than you were!"

Foster laughed.

"That's right. Arlene was smart — for a woman. The exception."

"Well, you're ready to accuse a man on hearsay. The vigilantes are probably itching to hang him without a fair trial. Bert's thick with Dobbs and that crowd. I just think somebody ought to ask

Buck his side of it before . . . before . . ."

It was difficult for her to picture such a strong, manly person like Jess Buck hanging from the juniper at Belleville. She had only met him once, but she had been struck by his bearing, the fact that he had turned down her father's offer to hire him as a gunfighter. Obviously, the man had principles.

"If Buck was a killer, then why did he turn you down when you wanted to hire him?" she asked.

"I don't know. Maybe he's one of those who's stealing off the horses and cattle, running them down Wild Horse Canyon. They tracked him going that way yesterday."

"Yes, that's what Julio said. That's what bothers me."

Julio Machado had been the one who had brought the news about the manhunt for Jess Buck. Amy had thought that Julio was a little too pleased with the news, but had said nothing at the time.

"Well, maybe that's why Buck turned me down. Afraid we might get on to him."

Amy considered that theory. Maybe her father was right. Maybe she was all sentiment and intuition. Yet there were times when her intuition was the only thing she could count on. In Buck's case, she was sure that sentiment wasn't involved. She scarcely knew the man. Her intuition, however, told her that he was honest, that he could not be a thief and murderer.

"I'm sure we don't have all the facts or all the answers," she said lamely.

"Nor are we likely to find out anything more, since it appears Buck has hightailed it out of the country. He got what he wanted — eight thousand dollars, maybe more."

"Why would he kill Moses, though?" Amy asked.

"Maybe for his poke," said Julio Machado, as he came into the room. Amy jumped, startled, her hand jerking away from the fireplace stone where she had been leaning.

"Howdy, Julio," said Foster. "Just talking about that Buck feller."

"Must you always walk in like that, Julio?" Amy snapped. "A body can't hear you come up."

"Must be the Indian blood in me, Miss Amy." A faint smile flickered at the corners of Julio's mouth. "Sorry."

"It's all right, Julio," said Foster. "Now, what was that about Purdy's poke?"

Machado sat on the divan. He was as much at home at the ranch house as they were. Foster had always wanted a son. His wife, Arlene, had died five years before and he had been left with Amy, who was now a grown woman. Machado was the nearest Foster could get to having a son and he lavished affection on the man. Amy was sure that Julio took full advantage of her father's weak spot. Her own attitude toward the foreman was more complex. She knew that Julio was a capable man. He knew horseflesh, cattle, men. Yet while her father trusted Julio, she did not.

"Talk in town is," Machado replied. "Moses had considerable gold in his poke. They figger the *pistolero* murdered the old man for that reason."

"What do you think, Julio?" asked Foster.

Julio shrugged.

"Might be. The man is gone. He rode down Wild Horse Canyon. The outlaw trail."

"Were you one of the trackers?" Amy asked.

"Yes. I saw his tracks. They were not hard to follow."

"What about stock? Any gone. . ."

"Father!" said Amy sharply.

"We did not lose any stock last night or today. Two dozen head of cattle were taken while the man was here in the valley," Machado said, staring straight at Amy.

"You think Buck was responsible for that, too?" Amy stared back at Machado. "The rustling's been going on for some time. Before he even came up here to Holcomb Valley."

"Yes. A few head at a time. Now, I find out that not only the Circle Horseshoe lost cattle, but over fifty head in the valley since Buck was here. Maybe he laid low until now and made his strike, then pulled out. Don't you, Lucky?"

"I didn't know that many head were missing."

"We checked the count today. It is serious."

"Yes," Foster frowned. "We can't afford to lose any more stock."

The cattle thefts had been going almost as long as the horse rustling. Good men were hard to find in gold country. That was another reason Foster prized Machado so much. If the depredations on his stock continued, however, he would doubtless go under. He was heavily mortgaged and unless he delivered a certain number of cattle to the fall markets, he would lose everything. So far, he had managed to keep the worst of the situation from Amy. Machado, however, was fully aware of the treacherous waters Lucky was treading.

"We lost another hand today, too."

"Who?"

"Salinas. He got the gold fever, I guess. Took off with a pick and pan to upper Holcomb I heard."

"Well, I wish him luck," said Foster wryly. "We'll have to replace him. We're short-handed as it is."

"Might be better to . . ." Machado began, but then realized he might give away too much to Amy. He knew that she was being kept in the dark about the Circle Horseshoe's precarious position.

"What were you going to say?" Amy asked pointedly.

Before Julio could reply, they heard the loud creak of a wagon in the ranch yard, followed by the sounds of men talking in loud voices. Foster got to his feet. So did Machado. Amy walked with them to the window.

"What the devil . . ." Foster blurted.

"Looks like a bunch of the miners from Belleville," offered Machado.

"Whatever could they want here?" asked Amy.

The noises grew louder. Sounds of a drunken argument issued from the wagon, which was packed with men. Amy turned and went to a table behind the divan. She lit another lamp, carried it to the door. Foster, Machado and Amy stepped onto the porch as the wagon creaked to a stop. Amy held the lamp high, throwing a cone of light on the faces of the men in the wagon.

"Whoa up, mules!" shouted Greek George in a gruff, whiskey-rasped voice. He wrapped the reins around the brake, stepped down unsteadily. Men tumbled from the box rig.

"Hullo thar, Mist' Foster, Miss Amy."

George sported a black oily rope of drooping moustache. His face was wide and strong-jawed, with high cheekbones, a flat, surly nose. His twinkling blue eyes glittered in the light. He wore two six-guns, his large, gnarled, rock-wrestling hands never far from their butts. They were rusty 1858 Colts, but they managed to fire when he wanted them to, and he fired them often.

"We come to see Miss Amy," a man named Blackbird Johnson said. "Ain't that right, Greek George?"

"You boys are pretty likkered up, aren't you?" Foster said calmly.

"Why, we're a-celebratin' the Union," Johnson said. "Tomorry's the 4th of July."

"What did you want to see me about, George?" Amy asked.

George stepped forward, doffed his knit watchcap, a relic from days at sea on a merchant vessel.

"We need a Betsy Ross of the mountains," Greek George said. "Someone to sew us a flag."

"We brung you some materials, Miss Amy," Johnson said, stepping forward to stand alongside the Greek. "Where's that sack, Fultz?"

A thin, balking man came forward carrying a cloth sack. He reached inside and drew forth stripes of material.

"Why, boys, that's sweet," said Amy. "Wherever in the world did you get those things?" She looked at the material that Fultz held in his hand.

"Them there tinsel pieces we got from the gals' skirts over to the Palace," said Johnson. "They's to make the stars outen. We got the red and blue material from a bunch of the other miners. They's for the red strips and the blue back. And, uh, well, that white material's from a bunch of the women, ah, well, you know. . . ."

"Why, Blackbird," Amy beamed, "I do believe you're embarrassed. You mean this is from the ladies' petticoats. How nice!"

"Yes'm," glowered Johnson, while the rest of the men chortled.

"They's more'n eighteen stars go on that flag," said someone. "Accordin' to that feller back at the saloon."

"That fella, he don't know," said George tightly, his tongue thick with drink.

"No, now, let's not argue, boys," said Amy. "I'll be happy to sew your flag. I'll put all the stars on it that need be there."

A chorus of jubilant shouts greeted her decision. The men piled back in the wagon, drove off, swigging from bottles. Later, pistol shots went off like firecrackers.

"Starting the celebration a little early," Foster said, turning to go back into the house.

"It'll be ugly before it's over," Machado said grimly. "There's going to be a horse race tomorrow. And a bear and bull fight. Many wagers. Lots of whiskey."

"Yep," said Foster, striding to a chair. "Boys will be boys."

Amy, carrying the sack of cloth, closed the door and looked at her father.

"Seems as though men have their sentimental side, too," she said.

Foster snorted.

"Come on, Julio," he said, "we might as well have a drink while Amy sets herself to sewing."

Amy laughed quietly.

She knew she had scored a point.

CHAPTER SEVENTEEN

The Palace was raucous with early celebrants on the eve of Independence Day. By the time Greek George, Blackbird Johnson, and the others returned, the party was in full swing. Fiddles screeched, banjos thunked and rang, guitars twanged.

Bert Singleton roamed through the saloon, slapping men's backs, stopping to talk or listen to a joke. Slatter sat in one corner, aloof, watching the swarm of humanity with cold eyes. Laurie Whiston was nowhere in sight and several people wondered where she was.

George made his way to the bar, like a burly bear, his cohorts following in his wake.

"Where's the tenderfoot?" he bellowed.

"Over there," someone said, "talkin' to the ladies."

"Haw, pilgrim!" the Greek roared. "We found our Betsy Ross. She gonna make the flag. With eighteen stars!"

The corner of the room erupted with laughter and cheers.

"I beg your pardon, Mister Greek," said the tenderfoot, whose name was Reeves Lundeen, "but I believe you are in error."

One of the girls on Lundeen's arm giggled inanely. The other frowned. Greek George had a terrible reputation and everyone in the place knew it. Except of course, Mr. Lundeen, a slender, hawk-nosed man who affected the air of a Boston dandy, to most of the male patrons' disgust and to the delight of the women in the saloon.

"What dat you say?" George's eyes bulged. He strode toward the tenderfoot, his chest thrust forward menacingly.

"I believe," said Lundeen, oblivious to the danger evidenced in George's rolling gait, "that there are at least thirty-five states in the Union. There were that many when I left New York, but I believe that Nevada has been admitted to statehood since then, which would make it thirty-six."

"Ya countin' them secesh?" grumbled one miner, as bunches of men began crowding toward the two men at the center of the argument.

"Why, of course," replied Lundeen. "The South can't last much longer. We'll bring them to their heels and to their senses."

Tempers flared among the men. Those from Union Flat siding together against those luckless southerners who lived scattered throughout Holcomb Valley. Greek George paid no attention to the fresh argument, but waded still closer to the tenderfoot.

"I say dat only eighteen star go on dat flag!"

he thundered.

"Well, Mister Greek," said Lundeen, "if you want a true flag made in celebration of Independence Day, then you'd better put at least thirty-five stars on it."

"By gar . . ."

"I guess thirty-six would be more correct. After all, what's one more state among friends?"

George boiled over. His ugly temper, well-known in the valley, flared out of control at the pilgrim's impudence. The crowd, encircling the two men, as if by a silent signal, pulled away, leaving the two men squared off, facing each other. The two dance hall girls melted into the crowd. Lundeen swallowed, looked around. The silence engulfed him. Nothing had been said. Nothing had been done. But, he was suddenly, deathly afraid.

Lundeen opened his mouth to say something, but nothing came out. Instead, his eyes welled with salty liquid as he saw George's hand slap onto the butt of one pistol, draw it and point it straight at him. The lump in his throat rose still higher.

For just a split-second of eternity, he saw George's sausage-like finger squeeze the trigger.

Lundeen saw, or thought he saw, the orange flame spurt out of the huge opening in the barrel of the pistol. He saw, or smelled, or imagined, a cloud of smoke hurrying toward him like a thick gray wreath. Something smashed into his chest with a thudding, faraway pain. He felt enveloped in fog, or smoke. It seemed to him that the crowd had sucked in their breaths in one collective, simultaneous surge. He could feel his own breath being sucked out of his lungs at the same time that everyone inhaled.

Lundeen was not conscious of being driven backwards by the force of the lead ball, nor of crashing into a table and skidding onto the floor like a broken mannikin. Nor did he ever see the gushing well of blood that poured out of his chest for the few seconds it took his heart to stop pumping. A red stain spread across his dandy shirt, his vest and soaked through to his coat.

"Eighteen stars, by gawd!" muttered Greek George, holstering his pistol.

For a moment, no one moved. Then, everyone swung away from the dead man and George turned back to the bar, surrounded by cronies. Someone dragged Lundeen's body out the back door and another swept up the bloodsoaked sawdust.

The improvised band struck up a lively jig and the clink of glasses mingled with the muffled talk about the shooting. Soon, that topic died out and the noisiness increased as though someone had speeded up a hundred hurdy-gurdies, cranking out a thousand discordant sounds.

Upstairs, Laurie Whiston ignored the noise and continued to weep softly to herself.

Everything seemed so far away to her, of little importance. A lamp glowed faintly on the bureau and she could smell the damp grass of Holcomb through her open window. The damp smell tugged at her heart, drawing more sadness out of it. She could shut out the sounds below, but not the scent of the land that lay out there in the dark of night like an open grave.

She was feeling sorry for herself and she knew it.

Yet she could not share her emotions right now with anyone.

Bert had asked her why she didn't come to work and she had lied to him. Again. She had lied to him so much, to everyone, really. Not bad lies. Just lies that kept her secrets to herself. Evasions that isolated her from the corruption she flowed through like some voiceless wraith.

She felt like a ghost at times, shut away from people, carrying her silences in her mind until they shrieked into bone-numbing headaches that she smiled away, rather than turn to drink. Now, she wondered if it had all been worth it. The silence. The lies. The evasions. The terrible mask she had worn.

She walked over to the window, eased it closed, shutting out the scents of the earth, the valley.

She sighed, thinking of Vern Slatter knocking on her door earlier. He had been persistent of late, since it was plain that Bert had his eye set on Amy Foster. Vern had a mistaken impression. He thought she was in love with Bert, but that wasn't so. Bert had been . . . only an anchor, a security for her in a world of insecurity.

The mining camps, the muddy streets of towns, the hard journeys from place to place blurred memories, smeared windows in her mind. Cripple Creek, Cherry Creek, Hangtown,

Virginia City, the Sacramento, the American, the Russian, and now Holcomb Valley. Following a will-o-the-wisp dream that was not her own, but following, nevertheless, watching men grub and steal and kill — for the yellow gold in the streams, the rocks, the hills, the leather pouches.

Laurie sighed, shook her head as if to throw off her musings.

Suddenly, she heard a noise at her window.

Startled, she glided toward the door.

Again, she heard a tap on the pane. Her blood turned gelid. A single tap, like a small stone or a knuckle, on the glass. Goosebumps crawled up her arms, chilled her neck.

There was a narrow balcony outside. She heard it creak with weight.

Her eyes widened, focused on the bureau.

She went to it quickly, slid open the drawer.

Her hand darted under a pile of hankies and garters. She grasped a small .41 caliber pistol, drew it from underneath. It was loaded and capped. She grasped it desperately, turned toward the window, bracing her back against the bureau.

It was quiet.

She relaxed, moved toward the window, the pistol quivering in her hand.

"Laurie?"

A whisper outside the window.

Her flesh prickled.

"Who is it?" she asked.

"Buck. Jess Buck."

Just then, the shot from Greek George's pistol boomed from below. Laurie's throat constricted.

It was quiet for a long time and then voices drifted up from the saloon.

"Open the window," said Buck.

Laurie's eyes narrowed to thin slits.

"What do you want?" she asked coldly.

"Some answers. I hope you can give them to me."

Laurie waited a long time before she raised the window.

Buck stepped into the room.

"What's the matter, Laurie? You've been crying."

"That — that's my business," she said.

Her hand grasped the brass-framed pistol, a gambler's weapon, small, deadly at close range.

He stepped back, chilled by her coldness.

"I ought to shoot you dead right now," she said tightly. She raised the pistol, pointed it at his head. "You — you murderer!"

Buck felt something sink in his stomach.

The barrel of the small pistol looked black and deadly, bigger than its caliber.

"It's Purdy, isn't it?" he asked quietly. "You think I killed him."

She raised the pistol to eye-level, cocked it.

"Yes," she sobbed, "it's Moses Purdy! You murdered that innocent man in cold blood! They want to hang you, but that's too good for you!"

Buck saw that Laurie was half out of her mind. Her finger slid toward the trigger. It would take only a slight movement for her to touch the trigger and fire the pistol.

"Steady, Laurie," he said quietly. "Give me a

chance to explain first."

His words had the effect he wanted. Her arm wavered ever so slightly. That's when he moved. He ducked and leaped at her. His left hand drove up, slammed hard into her arm. He knocked the small pistol out of her grip. Laurie reeled backward, fell onto the bed. Buck's momentum carried him in the same direction and he fell atop her. She began flailing at him, trying to strike him in the face with tiny, balled-up fists. He grabbed her wrists, forced them downward.

"Easy, woman. Calm down and let's start over."

"Get away from me," she spat, her face livid with rage. "You — you killer!"

"I thought we were friends."

"Friends?"

"I thought we were. Kind of. We started out that way. Now, you've got me tagged as a killer and I haven't even had a chance to put my chit into the pile."

He relaxed his grip on her wrists.

"You're beautiful when you're mad," he said.

Some of the anger fled from her face, softening the lines. Her makeup had all been washed away with tears. Buck though she looked some prettier without it. She also looked younger than he had thought she was, not over thirty, perhaps. He could be wrong, but right now, she looked confused and helpless. The hardness was gone. Something soft and genuine had replaced it.

"All right, Buck," she said tightly, "I'll put it to you straight. Did you kill Moses Purdy?"

186

He released her wrists, looked at her steadily.

"No," he said. "I liked Purdy. He helped me. Matter of fact, I got some information I was hoping to share with him."

Laurie's eyebrows went up. Buck slid away from her, stood up. She sat up in bed, rubbed her forehead.

"I believe you, Jess. But who did kill him and tried to make it look like you did it?"

"I don't know. Moses trusted you. And you care a lot for him."

She looked at him hard.

He should have seen it before. Should have stumbled across it in San Bernardino.

"He was your father, wasn't he?"

"Yes," she sobbed, breaking down again. "He was my father and I loved him so much. . . ."

Buck went to her, took her in his arms.

Her body shook. She cried for a long time.

He realized, then, that if anyone found out that Laurie was Moses' daughter, she would be in extreme danger.

And, of course, everyone would find out.

At the funeral.

CHAPTER EIGHTEEN

Buck knew he had stayed too long. Dal Nickson was waiting for him. None of his business, but Dal had been one of the hands where Buck had worked when the kid was killed. He had not forgotten that Buck had tracked down his killers.

"Laurie," he said softly, "I have to go. But there's something important I have to tell you first."

Her fingers squeezed hard, dug into the flesh of his arm.

"I'm scared," she said. "Scared that I'll never see you again. That you'll be killed like my father. They'll kill you, you know."

"They'll try. I'm counting on it."

"What?"

"Somebody up here's had a free hand. Somebody who doesn't want to play his hand in the open. Maybe I can draw him out."

"They're smart."

"Maybe. Laurie, I checked all the mining records in San Bernardino, those filed in Holcomb Valley. Moses told me about the Lost Star. I filed a claim on it. In my name and his."

"You what?"

"Wait a minute, now. The claim is his. I also filed a quitclaim deed. I think it might be the richest one up here. It's yours now."

"I — I don't understand."

He told her everything he had learned in San Bernardino. She listened raptly, her eyes brimming with fresh tears.

"Any reason you know of why your father didn't file on that claim?"

"He — he said he did."

"Yeah, that's right. He told me the same thing. But I think he filed on the wrong claim. Deliberately. And, someone else knows about it. Now, he'll know I filed on it, if my hunch is right. I may be able to smoke him out in the open."

"Him?"

"Or them."

"But you don't know who it is?" she asked.

"I have an idea. A strong idea. But I'll have to prove it. If I can do that, I'll clear my name and find out the truth about the Lost Star mine."

"Everyone here talks about it. I don't believe there ever was a Lost Star mine."

"Then a lot of people have died over nothing, Laurie. Including your father."

He took out a cheroot, bit the end off.

"Don't say anything about this, Laurie." He reached inside his shirt, pulled out an oilskin pouch tucked deep behind his belt. He handed it to Laurie.

"What's this?"

"The claim, the quitclaim, the deed transfers. They're yours now."

Before she could say anything, he was gone.

Buck had heard the shot from inside the saloon before seeing Laurie. Now, the street outside was quiet. He thought that odd, since he would have expected people to be streaming in and out. The hotel lobby was empty and the noise from inside the saloon spilled into the street. Business as usual.

Dal Nickson wasn't where he was supposed to be, across from The Palace.

Jess's scalp began to prickle. The hackles rose on the back of his neck.

He stayed to the shadows, walked across the street to the Assay Office. The windows were dark. He couldn't stay there long. He was an open target on the street.

The falsefronts, the cabins down the street, the butcher shop, were all dark. He heard distant laughter from the cabins out on the flat. The celebrations were going on all over. *But not in town. Not here.*

"Jess, dammit, look out . . ."

Buck went into a crouch, his hand streaking to his pistol butt.

Dal staggered into the street from between two buildings. He started to run, looked behind him as if fleeing from someone. His holster was empty, his shirt torn. His face, as he passed a cone of light from the Palace lobby, was ripped open at the cheek, one eye blistered shut.

Shots boomed from a building down the street.

Behind him, another shot.

Orange flame sprouted from two different directions.

"Jesus, Jess, they . . ."

Dal never got to finish what he was going to say.

Soft leaded balls cut him down, ripped into his back and side, jerking him off-balance. Another shot boomed, and Dal twisted sideways, propelled by the force of the ball.

Buck jerked his pistol free of its holster and hammered back in some smooth motion.

Still another shot blasted the night. Wood splintered from a post six inches from Buck's ear. He saw the dazzling red-orange flame, the billow of white smoke. From the crouch, he squeezed off a shot at the light that still danced in his eyes.

He heard a groan.

A man staggered from between two buildings. His legs crumpled. He fell.

Then, Buck wheeled as he heard pounding footsteps in the gush of silence. Footsteps — and another sound.

The jingling of coins in a man's pocket. Metal clacking against metal with a distinctive ring.

He started after the running man.

The jingling stopped.

A moment later, he heard leather creak and a hoarse voice. Then, hoofbeats that finally faded away.

Buck stared into the darkness, feeling help

less and alone.

The other shooter had escaped, but he knew who he was.

Jingles.

Buck did not know the man he had killed.

Dal was stone dead. There was nothing he could do for him.

Men crowded into the street now that the gunfire had stopped. Buck melted through them, his pistol holstered, his shoulders hunched. His jaw was set hard, and he tried to quell a pain in his chest that burned like fire.

There had been too much blood. Too many good men gone down. Dal, Turk, Moses. The bastards. He could not rely on anyone else. Not any more.

They must have seen him and Dal walk into town, jumped him while he was waiting. If so, then they had known he was upstairs with Laurie Whiston. Someone had cleared the street.

Who was powerful enough to do that?

Buck knew the answer.

Singleton.

With help from others.

There was a bitter taste in Buck's mouth as he stalked down the empty street, catching his breath. The fire in his chest subsided, the tenseness flowed out of his muscles.

He knew he could no longer play the waiting game. Every trail he had taken lately had ended in death. From now on, he vowed, every path he took would be direct.

Dal and he had been careful. They thought. They had hidden their horses and supplies in the rocky, pine-stippled hills between Union Flat and Belleville.

He had wanted to look up Kevin Whitaker, but that would have to wait. Tonight, he would sleep under the stars, in a dry camp. He would lie low tomorrow and come into town after dark.

The walk across the meadow was the only precarious part of his return to the hiding place. The lights of the town, burned in lamps by the 3000 souls who lived there now peppered the darkness with fireglow, receded, diminished, as he drew nearer the rock-strewn hillocks beyond the flat meadow.

No one was following him.

There were questions nagging his mind.

Something way back in his brain clawed for recognition.

Every time he thought of it, his mind focused on a single expression.

Pistolero.

Singleton had used that term. Called him that.

No one had called him that for a long time.

But Singleton had used it — *as if someone had told him that Buck had been called that a long time ago.*

A cold north wind jarred Buck awake before dawn.

He awoke, shivering in his bedroll.

It was time to move.

He circled the camp before leaving, checking for fresh tracks. There were none. In the half-dark he rode beyond the creek, leading Dal's horse behind his own, past any possibility of running into diggings. He angled toward a route that would allow him to double back to the Purdy claim.

The wind died down by mid-morning. Buck checked Purdy's cabin. He found fresh claim stakes on all four corners of the property. He had figured that much. The men he was after moved fast. And, they'd find a surprise waiting for them when they tried to file on the mine. He had expected that, welcomed it. In fact, someone was probably filing that very day. Which was all to the good. He wanted things to come to a head.

Satisfied, he rode in the general direction of the Foster ranch. He ate a lunch of hardtack and dried beef, washed down with creek water. He didn't want to arrive at Foster's before dark, so he rode off into the thick woods beyond the Van Duzen Trail and slept through the afternoon.

He ate a light supper of canned beans, peaches and jerky, then rode on. He had some hard questions to ask Lucky and his daughter, Amy.

No one challenged him when he rode up to the main house.

Amy Foster answered his knock, stepping out onto the porch when she saw who was there.

"Step down, Mister Buck," she said, "if you've business here. You can tie up your horses to the rail there."

"I have business. With you, and your father."
He swung out of the saddle, tied both horses to
the hitchrail.

"My father's not here," Amy said, as she ush-
ered him inside the house. He followed her to the
study.

Buck sat down, careful to avoid Foster's big
cowhide chair. Amy sat near him. He detected a
look of wariness in her dark brown eyes. Her
black hair was pulled back becomingly, her
cheeks rosy in the lampglow. The dimples at the
corners of her mouth were not there. Her lips
were set in a tight line. He took off his hat,
perched it on the toe of his boot as he crossed his
legs.

"Where is your father?"

"At his regular monthly meeting."

Buck's eyes flickered.

"Machado there too?"

"Why, yes, as a matter of fact. He always ac-
companies my father."

"Who's he meeting with?"

"Mister Buck, you seem to be asking a lot of
impertinent questions. I don't really think it's any
of your business. Besides, I don't know."

"Ease up, Miss Amy. I mean no impertinence.
Instead, I came to warn you and your father."

"You? Warn us? Of what? The whole valley's
up in arms about you, hunting you, and you ride
in here to warn *us?*"

"Miss Amy, please. Let's get things straight.
I'm no outlaw. Nor a gunslinger. Someone's
mighty anxious to get me strung up and I'm try-

ing my best to find out why. And I think I've got the answers. I think your father and Machado are meeting Bert Singleton. I think Singleton's using your father. And, it could be that he is in danger."

"I — I don't understand."

"Your father's involved in several murders and some shady doings."

She reacted as if he'd slapped her face.

"My father wouldn't be involved in any. . . ."

"Oh, he's involved all right. I have evidence that I gathered in San Bernardino that shows Singleton's got his finger in every pie up here. And your father's name keeps coming up, too."

"I ought to throw you out of here."

"Not until you hear me out. Singleton has a habit of acquiring claims after something bad happens to the original owners. Your father is losing cattle and I think he's being set up — for an 'accident.' "

"How dare you frighten me this way," said Amy, her brown eyes blazing with a fierce light. "You're as much as accusing Mister Singleton of stealing our cattle."

"Well, I ran across some papers that show him owner of a wholesale meat company in San Bernardino, and when I checked bills of lading, I learned he also bought beef from his own cattle company. And, nowhere could I find where he runs a single head of beef anywhere in these mountains."

Amy stood up, anger flushing her cheeks.

"I'll ask you to leave our house this minute, Mister Buck. I won't hear another word."

Buck stood up, towering over Amy. She seemed on the verge of striking him.

"One thing, Miss Amy, before I go. Can you give me the dates of the cattle thefts? It's mighty important. I'm sure your father has kept records. . . ."

"I don't see that that's any of your business, either."

"All right, but I wrote down the dates of all of Singleton's beef transactions from Holcomb. You look at them, check those dates against the dates of your father's regular monthly meetings. I'll wait."

He fished out some notepapers, handed them to Amy. He had others, which he stuffed back inside his shirt.

He stood there, staring her down, his eyes steady on hers. Without a word, she whirled, went over to the rolltop desk, opened it, pulled out a drawer. She pulled out a ledger, began leafing through it.

"Wh — what does this mean?" she asked, turning to face him.

"I think Singleton's men are going to drive off more of your cattle tonight. The foreman's gone. Your father's gone. It should be obvious. Bert Singleton is behind the rustling, just as he's been behind most of the dishonest doings in this valley."

"But . . ."

"If it's any comfort, Miss Amy, I think your father was taken in by Singleton. But if he ever suspects that you or your father have put two and two together, well, I think he would stop at nothing. There's too much at stake. Singleton is in too deep now."

"I — I don't know what to say. It's all so — so sudden."

"Just tell your father what I told you. Let him do some checking. I'll be back."

He left before she could say anything more.

Buck had some riding to do.

CHAPTER NINETEEN

Buck rode up to the back entrance of the stable.

Lantern light threw an orange circle outside. He heard the rustle of a man walking through hay, forking it into feed bins. He dismounted, led Dal's horse through the open doors, leaving his ground-tied outside.

"Whitaker?"

Kevin jumped, startled. He held a forkful of hay waist high.

"Mis — Mister Buck! You oughtn't be here!"

"Easy, Kevin. I want you to board this horse. It belonged to the man who was killed out here last night."

"They're sayin' you — you . . ."

"I know. That I killed him. Not so. Can you take me at my word?"

"You're takin' an awful chance just bein' here, Mister Buck."

"I need some information. That's all. Well?"

Buck extended the reins of Dal's horse to the youth. Kevin shook his head, shrugged.

"All right," said Whitaker.

He dropped the pitchfork, put the horse in a stall, stripped him down, pitched a forkful of hay into the feed trough.

Buck stayed in the shadows, waiting.

Frogs twanged deep chords in the meadow and bats whistled just outside the loft window, whispering past on leather wings. The aroma of sweat, hay, urine and grain permeated the close air of the stable. From down the street came the mournful wheeze of a squeeze-box playing *Sweet Betsy from Pike*.

"You said you wanted to ask me somethin'," Whitaker said.

Buck stepped out of the shadows, beckoned to Kevin. He took a cheroot from his pocket, hunkered down. Kevin did the same. Buck cleared hay away from the dirt, took a straw and inscribed a circle in the earth.

"I want you to think real hard, Kevin. I'm going to give you some names and ask if you've ever seen these men together. All at the same time."

"O.K."

"First of all, anyone ask you about Jensen?"

"Yep. Lots of people. I told them how it happened. And Billy Holcomb, he come up and took a . . . a depo something."

"A deposition."

"Yep. That was it."

"Singleton talk to you?"

"No. But . . . ."

"Slatter?"

"Yeah. He asked me. Got mad too. Said I was a fool kid, didn't have any brains."

Buck laughed quietly.

He scratched a thin line in the dirt.

"You have brains," he said. "Now, here are the names of the men I want you to tell me about. Singleton, Slatter, Lucky Foster. Ever see them together. And, if you did, who else was with them?"

Kevin took a deep breath.

A bat whipped through the stable, overhead, dove at a cloud of gnats that swarmed near one of the lanterns hanging from a post.

"I can't remember seeing them anytime special. I—I never thought about it."

"Think about it now," Buck said quietly.

Kevin frowned, then widened his eyes.

"One day a bunch of them come in with their horses all lathered and mudsplattered. Had me to clean 'em up. Hooves all caked with the same kind of red clay. It was just after a rain and those horses looked like they'd been sloggin' through some powerful mud holes."

"The men, Kevin, who were they?"

"Oh, they was a bunch of 'em. Bert Singleton, he was one. Vern Slatter, and uh, Lucky Foster, and. . . ."

Dal's horse nickered. Buck's answered, from outside.

Buck tensed as he heard a sound from in back of the stables.

Kevin looked up, past Buck's shoulder. His eyes bulged.

". . . and who?" asked Buck.

His words were blotted out in a sudden thunder.

Buck saw Kevin's face explode.

Blood sprayed from the back of the boy's head as the lead ball tore out a knee-sized chunk of skull. Kevin's forehead collapsed. He fell backward, lifeless as a rag doll, his eyes dulled by sudden death.

Buck whirled on the balls of his feet, drew his pistol.

The cheroot dropped from his mouth.

Smoke, white as a cloud, hung in the air by the back doors, swirling in the lamplight.

Buck got to his feet, raced outside.

At the edge of the dim light; he saw a man spring to a horse, gallop off across the meadow. Buck cursed, holstered his pistol. There wasn't a damned thing he could do about Kevin. The youth was dead, cut down as he was trying to say something.

Buck's horse was loose, frightened by the pistol shot. It took Buck several moments to catch him up, mount him. Behind him, he heard voices, shouts. He rode hard across the meadow, past the silent arrastres, away from the cluster of cabins.

Kevin had been about to say another name.

Yet he had asked *"What?"* instead.

No, not *what. "Who?"*

Who. The answer leaped into Buck's mind. It had been there all the time. He just hadn't seen it. It wasn't *"who,"* but the first part of a man's name that Kevin had been trying to say.

A Spanish name.

Julio.

Hooleeo.
Julio Machado!

Buck wasn't surprised that the horse and rider he was following headed straight for the Foster ranch.

He didn't press it. Let the rider think he was safe.

There was no question in his mind now. He knew who the rider was. He knew it all now.

He rode past the Foster ranch. He had to be sure. One more piece to fit together and then he would go after them. Every one of them. Starting at the top.

The Indian burial grounds loomed up in the dark.

Buck rode past, straight for Wild Horse Pass.

He heard them long before he drew near. The bawling of cattle, the scream of horses.

He caught up to the horses, a string of dark shapes, backs lit by soft pewter moonlight. Outriders flanking them expertly, moving them through the pass with the clattering, rumbling cattle.

Buck drew up into a clump of pines, some distance ahead, flanking the line of rustled animals. Fifty yards away, he saw a cigarette glowing orange in the dark.

"That you, Vern?" a voice behind the cigarette said.

Buck froze. The man seemed to be looking straight at him.

"Hell, you ain't . . ."

The ball whistled by Buck's head. He heard the explosion, saw the belch of flame from the rifle's muzzle. Fifty caliber. One shot. The man had shot his wad. Buck didn't wait for him to go for his pistol. With a wild rebel yell, he charged the man, drawing his Colt. Somewhere nearby, he heard hoarse shouts, then the jingle of a man's spurs. Or was it spurs? The sound was familiar. Buck fired pointblank at the rifleman, saw him throw up his hands and go over the cantle.

Men rode out of the shadows, firing pistols.

One of them jingled as he rode.

The air filled with leaden hornets, flashes of red-orange fire.

Buck wheeled, avoiding the stampeding cattle that fanned out in all directions. The scream of horses mingled with the angry shouts of men, the ragged roar of gunfire, the crack of branches snipped off by lead balls. He holstered his pistol, streaked for cover, zig-zagging his horse with deft use of the reins and his single-bit spurs.

He put trees behind him, raced across open patches of ground. The shouts faded away behind him. The gunfire stopped and a great silence filled the night.

It would take them most of the night and part of the morning to round up the scattered cattle. Men would be working red-eyed in the dawn and past.

Buck pulled up, rested. His side ached from the run. He let the horse blow. He listened. They might send one or two after him, but that wasn't

204

likely. They had their hands full. A dead man to explain or bury.

Reep had been one of those shooting at him, he knew. Vern Slatter probably another. Singleton's men. He wasn't surprised.

And, from the size of the herd, both horses and cattle, Foster must be near cleaned out. The final nail in his coffin. Or was it?

Buck rode toward the Foster ranch. Something didn't quite ring true.

Had he missed something, after all?

Buck tied his horse to a pine well away from the ranch house. He proceeded on foot to a point where he could watch the front door without being seen. Unless he missed his guess, he would not have long to wait.

He heard the hoofbeats long before the riders arrived. There were two of them.

They rode up to the bunkhouse yard, their horses lathered, wheezing for breath.

It took an extra effort on Buck's part not to throw down on them right then and there. But, he had to know for sure.

"Julio!" called Slatter. "Better come out."

The door opened. Julio Machado came out, lantern light spilling out the door at his back.

"Vern, you know better than to come here."

"Hell, Julio, Buck just jumped us. Killed Dobbs."

"Dobbs dead?"

"Yeah, and Buck got away."

"We thought you might want to get him," said Vern Slatter. Buck could see their faces clearly. The other man sat his horse, jingling change in his pockets.

"He was here, too," said Machado. "Better check with Bert. Seems Purdy left an heir."

"Oh?"

"Laurie Whiston's his daughter. And Buck filed in Purdy's name."

Jingles Reep muttered an oath.

"Jingles," said Slatter, "you should of got him tonight."

"It was too damned dark," said Jingles quickly.

"I want both of them," said Julio. "Tonight."

"The gal too?" asked Slatter.

"Yes, but I want the *pistolero,*" said Machado. "He's mine."

Now Buck knew for sure who the fourth man had been. Machado. And the years fell away like pages in a book. There it was again. That word. Following him from Texas to California.

Pistolero!

The three men rode away. Buck started for his horse, when a sound startled him. He sucked in his breath.

"That's far enough, Mister."

Buck wheeled. Lucky Foster had a pistol aimed at his head.

"Thought I heard someone skulking around out here. Who was that with you?"

"I'm alone," said Buck. "But your foreman just

rode off with Vern Slatter and Jingles Reep."

"I don't believe you. Julio's in San Bernardino."

"Right now, he's on his way to kill Laurie Whiston, and me, too, if he can find me."

"You'd better come inside, explain all this."

"There's no time," said Buck.

"I'll shoot you dead."

Buck shrugged. He started toward the house. Amy came to the door, held a lantern in her hand.

"Who is it?"

"I've got him," said Foster.

"Mister Buck? Was that you sneaking up here?"

"Miss Amy, if I don't get to town a woman's going to die."

"Button your lip, Buck," said Foster. Buck felt the pistol barrel in his back. Foster shoved him inside. Amy, wide-eyed, followed the two men into the den.

"Now, you've been here twice today. Those papers you left Amy. Where'd you get them?"

"I copied them out of the record books."

"Smart. What do you make of it?"

"Singleton's out to ruin you from the looks of it. Which is mighty strange, considering you're partners."

"Partners?"

"Looks that way to me, Foster. Secret partners. Those aren't the only papers I looked at."

"Oh?" Foster's eyebrows went up. He pooched out his mouth as if he were sucking a prune.

"Stock was issued six months ago. Legitimate

207

of course. In the name of the Bear Valley Mining Company. President, Theodore Foster; Vice-president, Bertrand Singleton. Secretary-treasurer, Amy Foster." His eyes shot to Amy's. She held her gaze steady.

"As you said, Mister Buck. All legitimate."

"Orders for stamp mills, dynamite, hydraulic equipment, ore cars, wagons. Pretty big venture, Foster. And no mining holdings big enough to support it."

Buck let it sink in.

"We have the mines," said Foster lamely, suddenly not so sure of himself. His pistol wavered.

"The incorporation papers list some mining claims that are not backed up with ownership papers."

Foster's face ruddied slightly. He seemed to be drawing on hidden reserves of calm.

"Go on," he said.

"I filed on the same claims in question. In Moses Purdy's name and in my own. I think one of them is the Lost Star Mine."

"The Lost Star mi . . ." Amy blurted before a look from her father withered her to silence.

"Ring any bells, Foster? If you were told by Singleton that Bear Valley Mining owned the deed to that claim, then you were hoodwinked. Pure and simple."

There was a long moment when Foster said nothing.

"It appears," he said finally, "that I have been taken in Mister Buck. I thank you for informing me."

"Ah, there's one more thing, Foster."

"Yes?"

"It appears to me that the last of your cattle and a right good string of horseflesh is heading for Cajon Pass at this very minute."

"I — I don't understand . . . Machado . . ."

"Machado's in on it. Vern Slatter and Jingles Reep work for him. And he probably works for Singleton."

"You said Machado is looking for Laurie Whiston. Why?"

"He's going to kill her. She was Moses Purdy's daughter. Legal heir. She works for Singleton, too. But she's not onto his dirty work nor a part of it."

"What are you going to do?" asked Amy.

"If your father will take that gun off me, I'm going to try and stop three men from killing an innocent woman."

The pistol came down.

Buck touched the brim of his hat, loped for the door.

What bothered him now was that Foster hadn't seemed at all surprised.

He wondered what he was telling Amy now.

CHAPTER TWENTY

It took Buck over an hour to come up behind The Palace. He knew he could not go to the stables, nor could he risk riding up the main street at that late hour. Machado and the others had gotten a good lead on him, he knew, and he'd had to tie his horse in the rock hills and walk on wobbly boot heels across the meadow. He had skirted the mining shacks, run from barking dogs, knowing he was probably too late to warn Laurie

He looked up, saw a light in Laurie's room. The stairs were empty, the balcony deserted.

It was quiet, except for the music and laughter coming from the saloon.

Maybe he had beaten the killers there.

He climbed up the back stairs, careful to step near the edges of the boards so that they would not creak so loudly.

He tiptoed toward her window.

Inside, he heard muffled voices. A chair scraped. He winced as he heard a slap, the smack of a hand on someone's skin. Men's voices. A whimpering feminine tone underneath.

Buck slipped his pistol from its holster.

He heard a low scream, then sounds of a scuffle. The screams choked off, as if someone had been gagged.

"No!" yelled Laurie.

Buck dove through the open window, his eyes wide open, his pistol firm in his hand, uncocked.

Slatter was trying to drag Laurie out the door. Reep was reaching for one of her arms.

Jess took everything in at a quick glance: the welts across Laurie's face, her swollen, bruised cheekbone, Slatter's slack mouth, glittering eyes. Jingles clawing for his pistol.

Buck crashed into the table that was strewn with the papers he had left there earlier. He slid halfway under it.

"Get him Jingles," hissed Slatter.

Laurie stared at Buck in stunned amazement.

Jingles drew the pistol free of his holster. He was lightning fast.

His face twisted into a snarling mask.

Slatter shoved Laurie down against the floor. Hard.

Buck cocked his Colt, squeezed the trigger.

His aim was true.

The lead ball drove into Reep's gut just above the belt buckle. The impact drove him back as he triggered off a shot. His bullet plowed into the table, inches from Buck's face, ripping a furrow through the wood.

Slatter drew his own pistol.

He ran forward, kicked the table into Buck. A

leg on the table snapped. Buck fired again. The table teetered over, caught the slug. A chunk of wood flew through the air.

Slatter cursed, fired pointblank at where he thought Buck would be.

Jess rolled, kicked at the rolling tabletop.

Slatter's bullet caromed off a nail, spanged into a porcelain wash basin. Water spat into the air like a miniature geyser.

Buck pitched forward, half-stood in a crouch.

Slatter wasn't ready for it.

Buck fired, aiming dead center for Vern's chest.

The gunman screamed in agony as the ball slammed into his breast. He staggered, trying to raise his pistol for another shot. A sliver of bone sheared through his chest wall, dripping blood. One of his lungs collapsed. Veins and blood vessels burst, sprayed crimson on his shirt.

"You sonofabitch," he rasped.

Mortally wounded, but tough as a boot, he brought his pistol up higher, grimly determined to take Buck with him to hell.

"Look out!" Laurie screamed.

Jess saw the man swim before his eyes. Saw a thousand sights before he squeezed the trigger again. He thought he was moving slow, but his reflexes were perfect, in fine tune. Hammer back, he squeezed as he stood tall, leaned into the target.

The ball shot straight between Slatter's eyes. His face collapsed in a cloud of blood. Brain chunks flew out the back of Vern's head, spattered the wall, dripped like grease on the wallpaper.

His eyes crossed eerily as the back of his head blew apart like an exploding bowl of mush. His pistol fell from his grasp, clattered on the floor. He toppled backwards, hit the floor with a sickening crunch.

Buck holstered his smoking pistol, tended to Laurie.

Her eyes smoked with terror.

That's when he saw the welts on her arms, the bruises on her face.

"They—they wanted me to sign over the claim to them," she said. "And—and then I think they were going to kill me."

"Come on, we can't stay here."

She grabbed up the papers, a carpetbag, while Buck reloaded. It had been quiet, but now the curious were beginning to make noises downstairs. They went down through the hotel lobby. People grabbed at them and Buck shoved them aside. There was no sign of Singleton or Machado. They raced outside, shouts following them.

"Run," he said, as they went around the building, came to the meadow. "Head for the rocks."

They raced across the meadow. Buck kept looking back to see if someone was following them. The voices died away. They reached the rocks out of breath. Buck helped Laurie up into the saddle, then swung up in front of her. She put her arms around his waist, the carpetbag dangling from her hand.

"Thank you," she breathed in his ear. "You

saved my life."

"It was my fault. I didn't think they'd go that far."

"Where are we going?" she asked as Buck moved the horse through the rocks and down the other side of the hill.

"To a place where you'll be safe."

"There's no place I'd be safe up here."

"Your father's cabin. That's where I'll have Singleton meet me tomorrow. Tonight, though, we'll be safe enough."

And tomorrow he'd play out the final hand.

Win, lose, or draw.

Before dawn, Buck slipped out of the cabin. He left a note for Laurie telling her when he'd be back. "Don't open the door until you hear my call," he advised.

He left a note at The Palace for Bert Singleton.

"If you want the deed to the Lost Star mine, meet me at Moses Purdy's cabin. I'll sell it to you for a price. Come alone." He signed it, tacked it to the front door.

Then, he rode hard to the Foster ranch.

Machado was packing up.

Buck rode up boldly, his shoulders square, his right arm dangling by his side.

"So, you come after me now, eh Buck?"

"If you want it that way. You going somewhere?"

Machado looked up at the tall man, his hands in plain view on the saddle cinches.

"You got Pentell. Dobbs. And last night you put down two of the hardest men I've ever known. Slatter and Reep. I don't want any."

"Was that you with them down on the desert?"

"No."

"You're the only one I know who would wear a California outfit."

"Is he?"

Buck turned in the saddle.

Amy stood there, dressed in bell-bottom trousers, a fancy shirt, tassled vest, polished boots. Buck's eyes narrowed and he thought back to that time when the fourth rider had stayed off in the distance.

Yes, it could have been. A woman. Amy Foster.

"Damn," said Buck.

Amy laughed and he saw the madness in her eyes then. She held a pistol, cocked, steady in both hands. The sights were lined up on him.

"Now you know," she said.

"No, I don't know."

"Bert Singleton and I are to be married. You don't know who I am, do you? Nothing familiar about me?"

"No."

Amy laughed harshly.

Her father came up, then, behind her.

"Don't, Amy," he said. "Don't tell him another thing."

Machado moved then. Buck was prepared for it. He dove from the saddle as Julio reached for his pistol. Amy's pistol boomed. A ball sizzled next to Buck's ear. He hit the dirt on the balls of his feet, snatched his pistol free of its holster.

Machado didn't make it. He knew he wasn't going to. Buck shot him in the belly, saw him go down, groaning.

Buck's horse blocked Amy from a shot.

Lucky grabbed his daughter, wrestled with her.

"No more!" he shouted. "Enough of this killing. You can't bring him back!"

Buck came around from behind his horse. Machado was finished, bleeding onto the ground, his eyes glazed.

"Leave me alone!" screeched Amy.

Buck watched the strange scene, his pistol still smoking.

"Amy!"

Amy was strong. She twisted her father around. He lunged forward.

"Look out!" Buck called.

Too late.

The pistol went off. Lucky stiffened.

Amy screamed, went into a swoon.

Buck grabbed her before she hit the ground.

Lucky thudded to the ground. He tried to say something. Blood bubbled up from his throat. He gagged, choked. His face turned purple, then blue. His throat rattled and he slumped into death.

Amy's forehead was clammy with sweat.

Buck slapped her to consciousness.

She stared at her father in horror.

Then at Buck.

He looked at her hard, then, and saw another face, a long time ago.

"It's not Foster, is it?" he asked. "Fowler?"

"Yes."

"Who was he? Your brother?"

"Yes," she hissed. "We were from Kansas. Norman Fowler was my oldest brother. I loved him very much."

"Never did know his given name," said Buck.

Billy Holcomb waved as Buck and Amy rode up. A sullen Bert Singleton sat on a stump, handcuffed. With Holcomb was Billy Edwards and Nick Tanner.

"Saw your note," said Holcomb. "Figgered to save you some trouble."

Edwards grinned.

Amy sulked, but her face was chalk white.

"Foster's dead."

"You mean Ted Fowler?"

"You know, then?" asked Buck.

"I've been digging too. I was right behind you all the way."

"Why?" asked Buck, looking at Amy.

Laurie stepped forward, glowering.

"People like her who don't have anything, want everything," she said. "You killed my father, didn't you?"

Amy lifted her head in defiance.

Buck shuddered. It was hard to think of someone so beautiful being so rotten inside.

"Amy Fowler, I'm arresting you for conspiracy and murder," said Holcomb, standing before her. "I'll have to put iron on your wrists?"

"What about Bert?" she asked.

"Already arrested him. He wasn't the smart one. You and your pa tried to make it look like you were victims and used Singleton in your scheme."

Buck saw it all now.

Edwards grinned at him.

"Wipe that grin off your face, Billy, said Buck. "No reason to gloat."

"Hell, we been tryin' to get those rustlers for over a year."

"Well, you got 'em."

Buck jogged his horse, turned it away from the cabin.

"Where you going?" asked Holcomb.

"Away."

"Need you to testify in San Bernardino."

"I'll be there."

Laurie rushed up to him.

"Are you leaving?" she asked. "This is the Lost Star mine, you know."

"I know. It was well named. It should have stayed lost."

"Will you come back?"

"Maybe."

His horse kept moving. He thought of Kevin Whitaker. A horse ought to have a name. This one had four white stockings. He would call it Socks and he'd call the blue roan, Blue. Good names.

"Goodbye Laurie."

"Wait a minute! Where can I reach you? Buck? Buck!"

But he was gone, weaving through the rocks, ducking under the pine branches. She ran after him, tears streaming down her face. She tripped on her long gingham skirt, stopped. She leaned against a rock, watched as Buck spurred Socks into a gallop.

Dust rose from the road, hung there until it shimmered in the sun, tiny gold motes dancing in the air.

Then, the dust settled and it was quiet for a long time.

BOLT BY CORT MARTIN

#9: BADMAN'S BORDELLO   (1127, $2.25)
When the women of Cheyenne cross the local hardcases to exercise their right to vote, Bolt discovers that politics makes for strange bedfellows!

#10: BAWDY HOUSE SHOWDOWN   (1176, $2.25)
The best man to run the new brothel in San Francisco is Bolt. But Bolt's intimate interviews lead to a shoot-out that has the city quaking—and the girls shaking!

#11: THE LAST BORDELLO   (1224, $2.25)
A working girl in Angel's camp doesn't stand a chance—unless Jared Bolt takes up arms to bring a little peace to the town . . . and discovers that the trouble is caused by a woman who used to do the same!

#12: THE HANGTOWN HARLOTS   (1274, $2.25)
When the miners come to town, the local girls are used to having wild parties, but events are turning ugly . . . and murderous. Jared Bolt knows the trade of tricking better than anyone, though, and is always the first to come to a lady in need . . .

Available wherever paperbacks are sold, or order direct from the Publisher. Send cover price plus 50¢ per copy for mailing and handling to Zebra Books, 475 Park Avenue South, New York, N.Y. 10016. DO NOT SEND CASH.

THE SURVIVALIST SERIES
by Jerry Ahern